THE HAUNTING OF HOLROYD HILL

"I hear something," Melinda breathed.

"Me, too," Dan said.

Kevin was silent. If this was a trick, it was a good one. He must have set it up beforehand, Melinda thought. She glanced at his profile. It was too dark to see his eyes but she had the feeling that he wasn't at all happy about the sounds they could hear clearly now, a shuffling, sliding sound. It seemed to be coming from the far side of the family room. Shuffle. Slide. Shuffle. Slide. It seemed to be getting closer.

And then she saw the light. It came ahead of the sound, a flickering, thin, yellowish glow, like a candle.

A tall dark shape came toward them. It wasn't walking exactly, though she could see the legs moving. It floated and shuffled and glided slowly, so slowly.

It looked like a man.

Slowly, agonizingly slowly, the shape moved across the room. The light came from a lantern it carried, a lantern with a single candle bobbing with its movements. Melinda wanted to scream but she couldn't seem to open her mouth. . . .

THESE PUFFIN BOOKS WILL REALLY CHILL YOU!

The Haunting
of
Holroyd Hill

Brenda Seabrooke

PUFFIN BOOKS

PUFFIN BOOKS
Published by the Penguin Group
Penguin Books USA Inc., 375 Hudson Street, New York, New York 10014, U.S.A.
Penguin Books Ltd, 27 Wrights Lane, London W8 5TZ, England
Penguin Books Australia Ltd, Ringwood, Victoria, Australia
Penguin Books Canada Ltd, 10 Alcorn Avenue, Toronto, Ontario, Canada M4V 3B2
Penguin Books (N.Z.) Ltd, 182-190 Wairau Road, Auckland 10, New Zealand

Penguin Books Ltd, Registered Offices: Harmondsworth, Middlesex, England

First published in the United States of America by Cobblehill Books, an affiliate of
Dutton Children's Books, a division of Penguin Books USA Inc., 1995
Published in Puffin Books, 1997

1 3 5 7 9 10 8 6 4 2

THE LIBRARY OF CONGRESS HAS CATALOGED THE COBBLEHILL EDITION AS FOLLOWS:
Seabrooke, Brenda.
The haunting of Holroyd Hill / Brenda Seabrooke.
p.   cm.
Summary: When her family moves to the Virginia countryside, eleven-year-old
Melinda, her older brother, and their new friend Dan work together to solve
the mystery of a Civil War–era ghost who is haunting their house.
ISBN 0-525-65167-5

Puffin Books ISBN 0-14-038540-1
Printed in the United States of America

For Kevin and Kerria

1

"Kev! Wait up, Kev." It seemed to Melinda that she had been saying those words all her life. Kevin was always running ahead of her, exploring on his own. When they were younger he ran ahead on purpose to get away from her because he was two years older. All brothers do *that*. But now he always seemed to be in a hurry to go places and to find things out. It was hard to keep up with him, especially in these dense woods. She could hardly see more than a few feet ahead of her. She must have lost him at that holly thicket. She had turned right to go around it. He must have turned left.

"Come on, Kev," Melinda called again. A bird gave a startled cry in the bushes beside her and flew away. She could hear the wing beats as the bird sped to safety overhead. The other birds were suddenly silent. Melinda didn't understand why Kevin didn't answer her. He couldn't be that far ahead. She had been with him just seconds before. Why couldn't he hear her? And why couldn't she hear him? Why did the woods seem cold all of a sudden? It was the middle of July in Virginia. A minute ago the woods had been hot and humid. Now it was more like November. What was going on?

Melinda called again. The woods seemed to be listening but there was no answer. Kevin could be quiet when he wanted to but not that quiet. This was an eerie quiet. Melinda expected to see a fairy-tale witch leap out at her any second. She wanted to get away from these silent, clawing woods. She jumped over a brush thicket but her ankle caught in a loop of vine. Her feet seemed to slip out from under her. She grabbed helplessly at branches and vines as she tumbled down a slope and landed on her knees at the bottom of a hollow.

The ground was soft with a thick padding of decayed leaves that cushioned her fall. Melinda examined her legs. She should have put on jeans when Kevin said he was going to explore the woods behind their house. But if she had taken the time to change, Kevin might have left without her.

It was warmer here in the hollow. She sat back to brush off the leaves. Her knees were dirty but unscathed. Melinda pushed herself up and felt something hard and knobby sticking out of the leaf pad. She dug it out and found a rock furred with green moss on the part that stuck out of the leaves. Melinda stroked its softness. She turned it over. The underside was slate colored with a thin line of white streaking across it like a ribbon. "Marble, I bet," she said aloud.

It was a keeper. Melinda stood up and slipped the rock into the back pocket of her shorts for her collection. A sudden riff of cool air made the hair on the back of her neck stand up as though an electric current had run through her. She put her hand on her neck but the hair there still tingled. She glanced up at the sun, screened by a thick clot of leaves. The light seemed to dim, though there wasn't a cloud in the sky that she could see. Melinda's skin prickled. She wanted to get out of this place *now*. She scrambled up the other side of the hollow and through the surrounding briery tangle that seemed to protect it like a fence. Melinda plunged through it, ignoring the thorns that grabbed at her bare legs.

Abruptly the brush thinned into what looked like a track. That must be what Kevin had found, she decided, and why he couldn't hear her call. He had found the track and gone running easily down it while she struggled through the woods. He could have come back and told her what he'd found. He didn't have to hog every discovery.

Melinda ran down the track ready to let Kev have it when she caught up with him. She rounded a curve and there she found her brother.

He was backed up against the trunk of a huge oak tree. His face was pale under his red hair and the few freckles across the bridge of his nose seemed ready to jump off and run.

He was facing a man with a pointed white beard and white hair. The man had fierce black eyebrows drawn together in a scowl over menacing dark eyes. He looked like the devil. In his hands he held a pitchfork.

It was pointed straight at her brother.

2

Melinda froze.

The man's scowl deepened when he saw her. He lowered the point of the pitchfork. "You kids stay out of my orchards," he said in a voice that sounded like it came out of the bottom of a well. "I know about you development kids. You think the country is an amusement park for your enjoyment. Well, it's not. So just stay out of my orchards."

He turned and stepped over a stone wall so overgrown with vines that Melinda hadn't even noticed it and stalked away through the rows of pear trees.

"I'm glad you came along." Kevin grinned, but his face was still pale under his freckles.

Melinda shrugged. She knew she hadn't been much help except that maybe the man thought it was harder to bully two kids than one. Well, it wasn't when one of them was her. She hadn't even been able to open her mouth to tell the man they didn't know they were in an orchard. She had been too scared. Her knees still felt like limp noodles.

"What a horrible man," she shuddered, feeling as though she had just swallowed a mouthful of spiders that were running around inside her. "He looks just like the devil with white hair."

"Except for those eyebrows."

Melinda stuck her hands in her back pockets. Her palm closed around the rock in the right one. It felt good and solid. She could have thrown it at the man. If she'd thought about it. Which she hadn't. Melinda wasn't good at confrontations. Unlike Mom, who was fearless and had a reputation as a ferocious opponent in a courtroom, Melinda hated unpleasant encounters. She could never think what to say or do. She always just stood silent and tongue-tied like she had today. Like a stone.

"Want to keep going down the track?" she suggested halfheartedly. She didn't really want to. She was afraid they would run into that man again.

"No. I'm thirsty. Let's go home and get something to drink. We should have brought something with us. If we had water bottles, we could keep exploring."

Melinda wasn't fooled. Kevin had been scared, too. He had lost his appetite for exploring today but he would never admit it. "I wonder where that man came from? I hope he doesn't live around here," she said as they headed home.

"If this is his orchard he probably does. He probably lives in that house in front of the orchard. You can see the roof just barely from our house." Kevin pointed ahead to the left.

Melinda looked at the dense green wall of trees and brush. She didn't see anything that resembled a roof. She hadn't noticed any house. And if there was one, maybe it wasn't that man's house. She didn't want to be neighbors with someone who looked and acted like the devil. "Maybe he lives somewhere else."

"He said *his* orchard. The orchard owner would live in the orchard owner's house. The mailbox is around the curve from ours."

Melinda hadn't noticed that either. But they had only been living here for a little over a week and most of her time had been spent putting things on shelves and helping organize the pantry and deciding where to put her furniture.

....

THEY made lemonade from a mix. Phil, their stepfather, was chipping away in the basement. That was one reason they had built this house, to give him room for his sculpture studio. When their mom's law firm in Alexandria opened an office in Broadfalls, she had become a partner in it. She said it was too far to waste time commuting, so they had decided to move. They were too crowded in their town house. This house was brand-new and roomy and in the country. "Think of the quiet," Mom had rhapsodized.

"Think of the mosquitoes," Kevin had joked. But he hadn't minded the move as much as Melinda. He liked rambling around in the woods by himself, exploring new places. She missed her friends Karen and Sarah and Caroline and their trips to the mall.

"They can come to visit," Mom had said, but Melinda knew it would never be the same. There was no mall in Broadfalls.

"I don't want to move to Holroyd Hill," she had complained privately to Kevin. He hadn't been sympathetic. His opinions of her friends were typical big brother opinions.

Kevin had had to leave his friends, too, but he would have

new friends any day now. You could put Kevin in the desert a hundred miles away from anybody and he would have new friends by suppertime.

Mom and Phil loved the new house. Mom had a home office that she planned to use a lot as soon as she got settled. Phil had the entire basement for his studio and planned to build a shed for his metal sculpture. He was already at work on a marble fish that an aquatic park had commissioned. Melinda and Kevin hardly saw him during the day except when he came up for lunch. With Mom away all day, they were on their own in the land of nowhere.

Theirs was the only house so far on Holroyd Hill Circle but others were planned. "It won't be long before you have lots of friends here," Mom said as they were unpacking.

"Maybe by the time I go to college," Melinda had muttered.

"It's only about six weeks before school starts and then you will meet lots of new friends," Mom had said as she unwrapped a mixing bowl and put it on the shelf of the new oak cabinet in the kitchen.

But for now Melinda didn't have any friends. Nobody lived near them except that awful man next door. She gulped her lemonade, angry that he had had the nerve to think they would take his old fruit. She didn't even like pears. She should have told him so. Now she could think of all sorts of things she should have said. She would write him a letter and tell him what she thought of him and his old orchard.

Melinda banged her glass down so hard on the sink she thought she had broken it. She stomped up the stairs and found the box of stationery her grandmother had sent her for Christmas. She looked at the folded notes with kittens playing in the corners. This was not the right paper for the sort of letter she was going to write.

Melinda got several sheets of computer paper and a long envelope from Mom's office and took them to her room. She sat down on her bed to write.

"Ouch!" The rock was still in her pocket. Melinda pulled it out and put it on the shelf with her rock collection—the geode Kevin had given her for Christmas, the shell fossil she'd found on Chesapeake Bay, quartz crystals, sandstone, granite, pink marble, pyrite, the desert rose from her grandmother, and others she'd picked up on school trips and vacations.

Dear Orchard Owner,
    My brother and I would never bother your old pears. We don't even LIKE them. We only like tropical fruits like mangoes and bananas and pineapples.

Sincerely,
Melinda Ryan

She folded the sheet three times and sealed it in the envelope. On the front she wrote: To the Orchard Owner.

Then before she could change her mind she ran downstairs. She went out the front door and down the driveway to the street and followed the curving circle to the place where a road led back through the trees to the peaked roof Kevin had said was the orchard owner's house. She could see the roof now, a shiny tin roof with a dormer window on the front under the roofpeak. An old rural mailbox leaned into the circle. Neat black-painted letters on the side read Sasser. Somebody had written in ballpoint underneath: Czernikow. Melinda opened the box and thrust her letter inside. She slammed the box shut and ran back home.

A boy stood at her front door ringing the bell. He was wearing a faded red T-shirt and khaki shorts and sneakers.

His hair was blond and shaggy around his ears. He carried a rolled-up newspaper. He turned around when he heard her on the driveway. His eyes were green and he was a little on the skinny side. He grinned and his face seemed to light up.

"Hi," he said, squinting in the sunlight. "Is your mom or dad home?"

"My dad is." Sometimes Melinda didn't feel like explaining that her parents were divorced and both remarried and that her father lived in Seattle with his new family. "Come on around this way." Melinda wondered who he was as she led him around the side of the house to the basement entrance. The doors were open. Phil was sitting at his drawing board in his summer uniform of khaki shorts, a T-shirt from his collection—this one had a scene from the movie *Casablanca* on it—and sneakers. There were marble chips on the floor but his block of marble was covered.

"Phil, somebody to see you."

"Hi, I'm Dan Czernikow." The boy unrolled the newspaper to the front page. "I'm the carrier for the *Broadfalls Weekly Gazette*. I have a complimentary copy for you to look over. We carry all the local news, opinion columns, editorials, ads . . ."

"You don't need to convince me, Dan. I'm Phil Markham and I'll be happy to subscribe. Local papers are the best way to get to know a community."

"Thank you, sir. I'll be delivering on Friday afternoons."

"You look about Kevin's age," Phil said. "Melinda, why don't you introduce Dan to your brother?"

"I'm twelve," Dan said.

"Kevin is fourteen," Phil said. "Melinda's eleven. Do you go to George Mason Junior High?"

"I'm almost twelve," Melinda muttered under her breath. "More twelve than eleven."

But Dan didn't hear her. "Yes, sir," he replied. "We'll all be on the same school bus."

Melinda squirmed. She was afraid Phil was going to say something really silly about how they could all be friends but he didn't. "Come on, I think Kevin is in the kitchen," she interrupted before Phil could say anything else.

Dan followed her. "Is your dad an artist?"

"Yeah. A sculptor. He teaches at Wakefield College in the winter and works on his own stuff in the summer."

"Cool. I never met a sculptor before."

Melinda never had either until her mom had married Phil. She wondered if Dan had a girlfriend.

Kevin was in the kitchen reading the comics in the *Washington Post*. Melinda introduced them. "This is Dan Czernikow from . . ."

"I live next door," Dan said.

Melinda stared at him. She must have heard wrong. He *couldn't* live in *that* house. "Next door? In the house way back from the road?" she asked, trying not to let her alarm show.

Dan looked at her. "That's the one. You can see the roof from the road."

But Melinda had to make sure. "The one attached to the orchard?"

"Yes."

Melinda looked at her brother. "I think we met your father or somebody," she said. "He had a white beard."

"Oh, that was Roy, my grandfather."

The man she had just written that letter to! Oh no! This couldn't be happening to her. This was the first friend she and

Kevin had made, the cutest boy she knew, cuter even than Billy Brown in her class last year. There probably weren't any other kids around for miles and she had just made an enemy of his grandfather.

"But how did you get here without me seeing you? I was coming up the circle," she said, hoping he would say that he'd come up the road from some other direction.

"I took a shortcut through the woods. We're new here, too. I mean, I am. My mom grew up here. We just moved here last spring from San Diego. My parents got divorced so we came to live with Roy because it's too expensive out there," Dan said, as though he was quoting somebody.

She had to get that letter back. Melinda edged toward the door. "Where are you going?" Kevin asked.

Why did he pick now to care what she was doing? Brothers. "Oh," she smiled brightly, feeling like an idiot, "I was going to get the doughnuts in the pantry. I thought maybe Dan would like one with some lemonade."

"Sure," Dan said. "I never pass up a doughnut."

Melinda got out the box of assorted doughnuts. She thought Mom was saving them for dessert but this was an emergency. There would be enough left over for tonight. She wouldn't eat any. "Get the lemonade," she told Kevin.

While their attention was on the doughnuts, Melinda slipped out of the front door. She ran all the way to the mailbox marked Sasser. Panting, she jerked the door open. The box was empty.

3

Melinda twirled the spaghetti around on her fork but she didn't eat it. She wasn't hungry. She didn't know if she would ever be hungry again after this afternoon. Besides, the noodles reminded her of things she didn't consider food. The sauce was too red and there were unmentionable-looking brown things in it that were probably only mushrooms but you never really knew. It was Mom's night in the kitchen. She didn't like to waste time cooking and never simmered the spaghetti sauce long enough. It didn't taste quite done to Melinda. Usually she put her plate in the microwave to cook for another minute or two but tonight she didn't want anything, not even her favorite foods, fried chicken or egg rolls or her grandmother's chocolate pie.

"You're not eating, Melinda."

"I ate my salad, Mom. It's too hot for spaghetti."

The air conditioning hadn't been turned on yet. Phil had designed the house as a low-energy user, his bit for ecology, he said. He checked the temperature in the house several times a day and was keeping a log. Each room had a ceiling fan with five broad white paddles that made a pleasant breeze. Melinda had to admit that so far the house had been comfortable. It wasn't exactly cool like their air-conditioned town house in Alexandria had been but she liked the fans.

"We were having doughnuts for dessert," Mom said. "But Kevin and his new friend got carried away and ate the whole box. I think there's some ice cream in the freezer. Chocolate ice cream should cool you off quickly."

But Melinda didn't want ice cream either. Kevin's new friend, Mom called him. Why wasn't he her new friend? He wouldn't be Kev's or her friend by tomorrow. She wondered what Dan's grandfather would do about the letter. Forbid Dan to come over here, she thought morosely. That would be terrible. The neighborhood didn't seem so isolated with Dan next door.

After she had been in bed for awhile Melinda was sorry she had refused the ice cream. Her stomach felt empty. She couldn't stop worrying about Dan's grandfather. Maybe he would forget about the letter. Maybe he had dropped it on the way back up to the house and it was now, at this very moment, disintegrating under a bushy rose vine. Melinda watched the ceiling fan circling lazily overhead. Raj, the golden retriever, snored softly below the window. The white curtains belled over him as a breeze pushed through the window. Her thoughts drifted. White roses floated on a green pool. The flowers turned into letters, then into birds that flew away when a wolf growled. She opened her eyes. It wasn't a wolf. It was her stomach. The bedside lamp was still on. She thought she had been asleep. Now she was really hungry. She padded down the stairs. The polished wooden stairs felt cool on her bare feet. She didn't bother with lights. She had already memorized the house layout.

Besides, there was a light from the kitchen. That would be Kevin hogging again. Phil said he had hollow feet. He'd better not eat all the ice cream. She knew who had eaten all those doughnuts. Dan had only helped a little. Kevin was a doughnut hog. Also an ice-cream hog. She hoped there would be enough for a bowl. Melinda went down the hall into the breakfast area and turned right to go in the kitchen. She prepared to pounce.

But when she reached the kitchen, it was dark and empty. Melinda switched on the overhead. The white counters were clean, the stainless steel sink gleamed.

Melinda took a bowl of ice cream up to her room. There were no sounds from Kevin as she passed the door to his room. How had he done it? The light had been in the kitchen when she was on the stairs. She'd seen it. But when she got to the kitchen it was gone.

....

"YOU were in the kitchen last night," Melinda said as she and Kevin ate breakfast at the redwood table on the back deck. He was eating cereal, thumbing through the morning paper. She had an English muffin smeared with black cherry jam.

"I wasn't," he said calmly over the rim of his glass of milk. Raj watched with pleading eyes. He loved anything that came out of a human dish. Melinda had once gotten him to eat a pickle by putting it on her plate.

Melinda didn't give up easily. "I had ice cream. What did you eat?"

"Nothing. I went straight to sleep."

"Um hum." She tossed a crumb to Raj who caught it in midair.

"You must have been dreaming. Or sleep walking."

"I never sleep walk. And I know what I saw."

"Which was?"

"A light in the kitchen. But when I got there it was gone."

"Car lights." Kevin crunched a mouthful of cereal.

Melinda hadn't thought of car lights. Of course, that could be the explanation. "Are you going exploring again today?"

He didn't answer. His nose was in the *Washington Post* comics.

Melinda got up to feed Raj. Mom always gave him a bone biscuit when she left for her office every morning and Phil saved him bits of toast but Raj always pretended to be starving when Melinda left the table. She poured dry dog food into his bowl. When she returned to the deck Kevin was gone. His empty bowl was on the table, the newspaper in his chair. It wasn't fair. He knew she had to feed Raj. He could have waited for her. She bet he was with Dan. Maybe Dan's grandfather had said he could only be friends with Kevin. "You stay away from that girl. She's a bad apple." That was probably the way an orchard owner talked. Or maybe he would say a bad pear. Her day was ruined. Her life was ruined. She would never have any friends again.

Phil was in the basement, waltzing with his fish, he said. Mom had left earlier for her office. Melinda had watched her leave from her window. She looked chic in a rose-colored knit suit and coral T-shirt. She waved and blew a kiss as she backed out of the garage and saw Melinda. Mom was working. Phil was working. Kevin had a friend. They were settling down to their new life in Broadfalls, getting into a routine. She was the only one with nothing to do.

She went to her room and rearranged her rock collection. The rocks were already dusty after only a few days. It was the ceiling fan and open windows that caused all the dust. She took them to the bathroom and washed them in the lavatory, drying them on a towel. She put the freshly washed rocks back on the shelf and looked for a book to read. She had read all of her books several times. Besides it was too nice outside to stay in. Melinda went out and sat on the edge of the deck and thought about the light in the kitchen.

She considered car lights. She couldn't rule out the possibility. But it didn't seem likely. For one thing she would have heard a car. There wasn't any noise on Holroyd Hill except insects. And for another the kitchen was at the back of the house. How could a car in the circle flash its lights into the kitchen? It couldn't. She decided Kevin was just trying to throw her off the trail. It had been Kevin in the kitchen. She was sure of it. She just had to figure out how.

She needed more clues. She would catch him tonight. He'd been successful in fooling her once and he would try it again. She knew her brother. But this time she would be ready for him. She would stay awake all night if she had to. He wasn't as smart as he thought he was. He wouldn't fool her again.

....

MELINDA woke up feeling hot and sticky, her nightshirt glued to her back. As her eyes adjusted to the darkness, she could see Raj, snoring gently, on the white rug on the floor beside her bed. She could see her rock collection, dark spots on the white shelves, rows of books on the other shelves. In the corner on the yellow velvet chair sat her rag doll, Gwendolyn, staring stiffly in front of her, her green dress held out by layers of petticoats. The luminous digits of the clock on her bedside table said 11:43.

Was that a noise? Melinda held her breath but she couldn't hear anything. She crept out of bed, tiptoed down the hall, and down the stairs. She could see a faint glimmer of light. It seemed to flicker but it was definitely a light. Melinda hurried. She would catch Kevin in the act.

She sped through the hall to the breakfast room and rounded the corner, ready to shout, "Aha! Caught you in the act."

The light was in the kitchen. Someone was in there. She could see a dark shape. But before she reached the doorway, the light seemed to fade into the far wall. Melinda switched on the kitchen light. The room was empty.

She had seen a figure. Melinda snatched open the door to the utility room and turned on the light. Nobody. She searched for hidden wires, anything that would explain the mysteriously disappearing light.

No Kevin. No wires. No explanation. Melinda raced upstairs to Kevin's room. She burst through the door. He was sprawled asleep across his bed, a stack of books he'd been reading piled on the floor. As she listened he made sleeping-Kevin noises, impossible to fake because he didn't even know he made them.

If Kevin wasn't responsible for the light, then who was?

4

"It wasn't me," Kevin insisted the next morning.

"It was. You rigged it up." There were no other explanations for the lights and the figure. Acceptable explanations, she amended. Burglar and ghost were two that hovered in the back of her mind. But she dismissed one as improbable and the other as silly without even considering them.

"How? How did I rig it up?" Kevin demanded, chewing a piece of buttered toast.

"I don't know yet, but I'll find out." Melinda had gone over the kitchen inch by inch in daylight but she couldn't find evidence of anything to explain what she had seen.

"Maybe it was a ghost," he said, grinning.

"What was a ghost?" Dan asked as he loped across the lawn and bounded onto the deck with one leap. He scraped back a chair and sat down.

"Melinda thinks she saw a ghost."

"I did not," Melinda protested. "I think I saw you or one of your tricks."

"I haven't done any tricks in years," Kevin said. "Not since the third grade. Anyway, why would I try to make you think you've seen a ghost?"

Boredom was the only answer Melinda had and she knew Kevin was never bored. He wasn't a mean brother either, even if he did go off with Dan yesterday, leaving her alone. A guy thing, he'd said. Nothing personal. But he liked to joke and play tricks. "If it isn't you, what could it be?"

"I told you. A ghost."

"How could it be a ghost?" Melinda scoffed. "This is a brand-new house. Ghosts don't haunt new houses. They only haunt old ones that are all musty and cobwebby and usually falling down. Ours is bright and smells like fresh paint and Mom's potpourri and lemon oil. Besides, I don't believe in ghosts."

"Want some breakfast?" Kevin asked Dan.

"No, thanks. I just ate. Roy made French toast this morning."

Melinda glanced at him. He didn't seem to know anything about the letter. Maybe his grandfather hadn't mentioned it. Maybe he hadn't told his grandfather he'd met her and Kevin. What was the worst thing Roy could do? He could tell her mother, but Mom wouldn't care. She believed in people standing up for their rights and was always encouraging Melinda to be more assertive. Roy might forbid Dan to have anything to do with her and Kevin. That would be terrible. But maybe he wouldn't do anything. Melinda hoped not. She didn't want to lose the only friend they had on Holroyd Hill.

"Why do you call him Roy?" she asked.

Dan shrugged. "I've always called him that. When I was little we lived near my father's parents. I called his father Grandaddy. So I called Roy, Grandaddy Roy. When we moved here I called him Grandaddy Roy a few times until he told me it was a mouthful and to call him Roy. Where did you see this ghost?"

"In the kitchen," Kevin answered for her. "She saw it Monday night and again last night."

"No kidding! My mom says that our house is supposed to be haunted. It's sure old enough. But I've never seen anything. She hasn't either."

"What about your grandfather?" Kevin asked.

"He's never said. He doesn't talk a lot, sort of got out of the habit. My grandmother died a long time ago. Mom says he was becoming a hermit before we came back to live with him."

Melinda was glad to hear that Roy didn't talk much. And he hadn't forbidden Dan to come over. Maybe he hadn't even read the letter. Maybe he really had lost it. Maybe he'd forgotten what it said. Maybe he didn't care.

"I think we ought to have a ghost hunt," Kevin said.

"Now? You can't have a ghost hunt in the daytime," Melinda objected. "If you did, you wouldn't find any because they only come out at night. Everybody knows that." What was she saying? She didn't believe in ghosts.

"Don't be stupid. Of course, I don't mean now. We have to make our plans now. We'll have our ghost hunt tonight," Kevin told her.

"But what about Dan? He wants to hunt with us, don't you, Dan?"

He grinned. "I never pass up a good ghost hunt."

"He can spend the night," Kevin said, as if it were all arranged.

Kevin took charge. They called Dan's mom at the library

where she worked and she gave him permission. Phil said it was OK, just don't bother him now because he was sussing out the marble, whatever that meant.

"Here's our plan," Kevin said later. They were in his room. Raj snoozed at Melinda's feet. "What time did you see the alleged ghost?" Kevin was going to be a lawyer like Mom. She said he already talked like one.

"I *never* said it was a ghost. That was you and Dan. I *said* something woke me up both times around 11:43."

"How do you know what time it was?"

"Because I looked at my clock right after."

"OK. We'll pretend to go to bed. At 11:30 you come to my room. We'll hide somewhere downstairs and lie in wait for the ghost to appear." He laughed fiendishly.

Melinda wished he wouldn't do that. What if they really did see something and Kevin wasn't doing it?

They watched TV after supper until Mom said it was time to go to bed. For once nobody objected. Melinda went to her room but didn't put on her nightshirt. She wanted to be ready for anything. She would catch Kevin this time if he was the ghost. She checked her clock. It was only 10:30. Melinda opened a book and stared at the print until it blurred. She was too excited to read.

At 11:00 Melinda began checking the clock every thirty seconds. She was supposed to go to Kevin's room at 11:30 but she decided to go five minutes early to interrupt them if they were working on a trick. She tiptoed to his room and pushed the door open, ready to say, "Aha! Caught you!" But they were only reading comics.

"It's time," she said.

They jumped up, ready to catch a ghost. Melinda went back

to shut Raj in her room. His toenails made too much noise on the bare floor.

"He might scare the ghost away," Kevin said, snickering.

The hall upstairs was carpeted in soft gray blue but the stairs were bare. Melinda thought their feet thudded like thunder on the polished boards, but Mom and Phil didn't seem to hear them. Their door was closed and no light showed under it. They were probably asleep.

Silently they filed into the breakfast room. They had decided to hide underneath the round table there where they had a clear view of the kitchen and the back of the house.

"That's where the ghost manifests itself so far," Kevin said.

Melinda felt a chill go down her spine. "Don't say that," she whispered

"That's the proper nomenclature," he whispered back.

"What?"

"Term. Name."

"Oh." Melinda still thought "Kevin's tricks" was the proper term for what was going on, but she took her place between the two boys on the floor beneath the table and waited.

"Everybody keep quiet now," Kevin ordered. "Ghosts like it quiet."

Melinda wondered how he knew what ghosts like. He'd never met one. If he had, she would have heard about it over and over and over. Like the time he saw the snake in Frying Pan Park. It got bigger and bigger and meaner until it was at least fifty feet long and chased him around the Washington Beltway.

Time seemed to slow down. Melinda felt her pulse throbbing. Her left shoulder blade itched, then her little toe and next her right earlobe.

"Stop fidgeting," Kevin hissed.

"I don't think it's coming," she said.

"It won't if you don't keep quiet."

Melinda opened her mouth for a retort but closed it again as her ears picked up a faint shuffling sound.

"I hear something," she breathed.

"Me, too," Dan said.

Kevin was silent. If this was a trick, it was a good one. He must have set it up beforehand, she thought. She glanced at his profile. It was too dark to see his eyes but she had the feeling that he wasn't at all happy about the sounds they could hear clearly now, a shuffling, sliding sound. It seemed to be coming from the far side of the family room. Shuffle. Slide. Shuffle. Slide. It seemed to be getting closer.

And then she saw the light. It came ahead of the sound, a flickering, thin, yellowish glow, like a candle. Melinda started to remind her brother that Mom and Phil had decreed no candles after Kev had burned a hole in a rug trying a scientific experiment when he was nine. But he was rigid beside her. Melinda followed his gaze and felt her heart lurch.

A tall dark shape came toward them. It wasn't walking exactly, though she could see the legs moving. It floated and shuffled and glided slowly, so slowly.

It looked like a man.

Melinda stopped breathing as she waited for the man to move on. There didn't seem to be enough air in the room anyway. When she could hold it no longer, her breath came out in a rush. Beside her, Kevin clutched her ankle. There was no sound from Dan. Melinda thought he had stopped breathing, too.

Slowly, agonizingly slowly, the shape moved across the

room. The light came from a lantern it carried, a lantern with a single candle bobbing with its movements. Melinda wanted to scream but she couldn't seem to open her mouth.

The figure passed without a glance at the three huddled under the table as though it didn't even notice them. It seemed intent on moving forward as it inched its way toward the kitchen and then through the doorway.

The shape reached the kitchen and melted into its shadows. Only the meager light from the candle marked its passage. And then it reached the other side of the kitchen and went through the wall.

5

At first nobody moved. Something was holding her ankle. Melinda tried to kick free. "It's me," Kevin whispered, letting her ankle go.

Dan had her wrist in both of his hands. She held his knee. Her other hand squeezed the tail of Kevin's T-shirt.

"He's gone." Kevin's voice cracked. It had been doing that a lot lately, mostly when he was excited or scared. He sounded like a frog.

"But where did he go?" Dan said.

"Through the w-w-wall." Melinda's teeth chattered.

She was in no hurry to leave the safety under the table, but Dan was no longer holding her wrist. She let go of the boys and crawled out of their hiding place.

Dan stood up. "Let's check the kitchen."

Kevin switched on the overhead light. The kitchen was safely familiar and bright as day under the glare of fluorescent lighting overhead. There were no lurking shadows, no shapes hiding, waiting to spring out at her. The refrigerator hummed quietly. The faucet gleamed in the light and the counters were wiped clean, just the way they had been left after dinner.

"How did he get through the wall?" Dan asked.

Melinda didn't have an answer. The light had disappeared the same way both times before. "I think that's where he went the other two times, too."

"What's behind that door?" Dan asked.

"The laundry room," Kevin said.

"Maybe we should look in there," Dan suggested.

They looked at each other. Nobody wanted to open that door. Melinda didn't believe there was anybody or anything in the next room. But she didn't want to open the door either. What if something was there? What if she imagined somebody there? That would be just as bad. Almost. She had opened the door before and nothing had happened. But that was before she knew there was a ghost in the house. Maybe it wasn't quite a ghost then. *Arghhh*. That was worse. Maybe he was waiting in there, waiting to spring on whomever opened the door this time. She looked at the boys.

"It's your house," Dan said.

"I'll open it," Kevin said. "Just give me a minute."

"That might be too late," Melinda said.

"All right, all right." Kevin took a deep breath and turned the handle. It seemed to take forever. The door swung open.

Light from the kitchen spilled into the laundry room, falling on the washer and dryer, the freezer in the corner. No one was there. Melinda giggled.

"No ghoulies or ghosties," she said to the boys.

They were quiet as they went back upstairs. Nobody seemed to want to talk about what they had seen. Or felt. Or experienced. Whatever it was. As she went to her room, Melinda thought the boys were lucky to be in a room together. She wished she had somebody besides Gwendolyn in her room. Raj was stretched patiently across the doorway. She left her door open and her bedside light on and snapped her fingers for Raj. He didn't need a second invitation but leaped onto her bed, grinning with delight. He loved to sleep with her but since he had grown up he took up too much room. She wouldn't let him when it was hot. But tonight she was glad to have him close. She put her arm around him and hugged him. His soft fur tickled her cheek. He sighed and instantly began to snore. Melinda was sure that she wouldn't sleep at all.

Raj was on the floor when Melinda woke up at seven. He always got too hot in her bed and crept out after she went to sleep. Her mother tiptoed in to turn off the bedside light. "Reading late again," she said with a smile.

She looked crisp in a pale green linen suit and soft white shirt, little square jade earrings, her blonde hair in a smooth French braid. She looked like a lettuce leaf. Melinda gave her a sleepy smile. "Your hair is still wet," she said.

"It'll dry in the car," Mom said as Melinda rolled over and went back to sleep.

....

"MAYBE we imagined it all," Melinda said, waving her toast crust. The bright morning sun made ghosts seem silly and improbable.

"You mean like a group hallucination?" Kevin said. He leaned back in his chair and hooked his feet on the deck railing.

"Listen, I know what I saw." Dan crunched his toast noisily. "I saw what looked like a ghost."

Kevin chewed a blueberry muffin and stared into the woods behind the house. He had made the muffins himself and forgotten to add sugar, so nobody else would eat them. Except Raj. "It couldn't have been a ghost," he said slowly. "There's no such thing." He sounded like he was trying to convince himself.

"I thought you were doing it." Melinda pointed her crust at Kevin and waved it like the wand he had used in his magic tricks when he was younger. He had never fooled her then. Well, not since she was about five. And he couldn't fool her now. He had been as scared last night as she and Dan. "I thought it was one of your tricks."

"If I could do a trick like that I'd be rich and famous," Kev said, tossing Raj the last bite of muffin. He gulped it down and stood in front of Melinda looking pitiful. She gave him her crust.

"It wasn't a trick. I think we can all agree on that," Dan said.

What they couldn't agree on was what it was. Melinda thought it was imagination. She hoped it was imagination, now that she knew it wasn't a trick. Kevin insisted it was an hallucination.

"Hallucination and imagination are almost the same thing," Dan said.

"Whatever it was, we all saw it," Melinda said.

"I think we should assume we saw a ghost," Dan said slowly. But Kevin wasn't ready to admit it.

"It's unlikely that all three of us would have hallucinated or imagined the same thing at the same time," Dan argued.

"We need to make notes and compare them. Then maybe we can figure out what's happening," Kevin said. He got pencils and a notebook from the kitchen and tore out a sheet of paper for each of them. "Everybody write down what you saw."

Melinda chewed her pencil. She could see quite clearly the figure moving through the house, shuffling, staring ahead, the bobbing light. But the figure was still in her mind. If she put it on paper, it would be real and that scared her. She didn't want it to be real. She wanted it to be one of Kevin's tricks. She glanced at her brother. He was writing furiously. She looked at Dan and he was looking at her. They both smiled. Dan gave a little shrug as if to say "It's better to face things" and started writing.

After a minute Melinda stopped chewing her pencil and began to write.

Dan finished first, then Melinda. Finally Kevin said, "OK. Let's compare. We all saw a light, right?"

"Someone carrying a lantern with a candle in it," Melinda said. "The candle flickered. If we were imagining, would we have imagined that?"

"I don't know," Kevin said. "I've never imagined a ghost. Now what about sound?"

"I heard a sliding sort of shuffling sound," Melinda said.

"Me, too," Dan said.

"That's what I heard, too," Kevin said.

"And it moved slowly," Dan went on. "It must have come in through the family room."

"There's no door in there," Kevin said. "It must have come through the wall." His voice sort of squeaked at the end.

"There's a chimney," Melinda reminded him.

"Yeah. Santa Claus getting his seasons scrambled," he retorted. "We don't know how it got in. Now the thing takes about five minutes to go from one end of the house to the other. Right?"

"It does move awfully slowly," Dan said.

"Like there was something wrong with its legs," Melinda said.

"That's an assumption. No assumptions," Kevin said.

"Maybe that's just the way ghosts walk. I mean we don't have anything to compare our ghost with."

Nobody said anything for a few minutes.

Then Melinda said, "You said ghost. Do you admit it was a ghost?"

Kevin cleared his throat. "Just for the purpose of this investigation. We can prove that it wasn't a ghost much more easily than we can prove it *was* a ghost. Now what else did we see?"

"I saw a man," Melinda said, still reluctant to give it human qualities.

Dan nodded. They both looked at Kevin. He looked uncomfortable.

"Yeah. I saw him, too. It was shaped like a man."

"It looked like it was wearing some kind of uniform," Melinda said.

"We couldn't see enough to tell," Kevin objected. "We have to be accurate. Possibly he wore a uniform. We need more information to find out what's causing this haunting now."

Haunting. It was the first time that word had been spoken. Melinda looked at Kevin. He clamped his mouth shut, as though he had just realized what he had said and wished he hadn't. Dan looked at the woods. His eyes had a faraway look. Melinda felt faraway, too, but not far like being in Mexico or Paris. It was a feeling of being far away in time, long ago. Kevin broke the silence.

"Monday night was the night Melinda first saw the light," Kevin said. "I mean why didn't it walk Sunday night or last Thursday?"

"We were up late unpacking most of last week," Melinda reminded him. "Maybe the ghost doesn't walk when there are lights on."

"Maybe. But one night, I think it was Saturday, I went down to let Raj out. He came to my room and breathed in my face, but when we got downstairs he didn't want to go out, so I gave him a treat which was what he wanted. I didn't bother to turn on the lights. It was just a little before midnight. I didn't see anything. So why Monday? What happened on that day to call up a ghost?"

Melinda shivered in the July heat. She and Kev had met Dan's grandfather on Monday. It had been an awful experience, but she didn't think it would cause a ghost to start walking through their house. Unless his grandfather was the devil. She didn't want to believe that.

What else happened Monday? She tried to remember. They came home and she wrote that letter and put it in Dan's mailbox. But she hadn't known then that it was Dan's mailbox. And she didn't want to think about that. Besides, it didn't have anything to do with the ghost. "I remember. We met Dan that day."

"Dan, did you bring that ghost over here?" Kevin asked solemnly.

"No, I did not. I keep my ghost collection at home under my bed. When I get enough, I'm trading them in for a werewolf. Or a vampire. Which do you think would be the most fun?"

"Be serious." Melinda laughed nervously. Could ghosts hear you when they weren't around? Could they hang around sort of spying on people? What a horrible thought.

"Yeah," Kevin said. "We have to be serious. We have a ghost on our hands."

"What I don't understand," Melinda said slowly, "is why a ghost is haunting our brand-new house. I mean, Dan's house has been here since when?"

"1842."

"1842. Why doesn't the ghost haunt his house instead of ours. I mean ghosts are supposed to haunt old houses, not new ones."

"Sometimes they haunt new houses if they are built over a cemetery," Dan said.

The sun blazed across the edge of the woods behind their house where the July flies made a sudden loud crescendo. Melinda felt as though somebody had just jerked her hard. The back of her neck prickled. Something was in those woods, around the house. Raj chose that moment to let out a loud mournful howl from under the table where he was sleeping with his eyes half open.

"Do you suppose he sees something?" she whispered. "Dogs do, you know."

They looked at Raj. His head lay atop his crossed paws. One lip hung down to the floor exposing his teeth. He seemed to be grinning out of one side of his mouth. As they watched, he yelped and twitched.

"No. He's just chasing rabbits in his dreams," Dan said.

"One more thing we have to decide on," Kevin said, "besides why the ghost is walking and why here and now, is what we are going to do about it."

Melinda knew she would never sleep again in this house as long as it was haunted. She had only slept at all last night because she was exhausted. She'd read enough ghost books to know what they had to do.

"I think we have to solve the ghost's problem, whatever it is," she said with much more confidence than she felt. "Otherwise, we'll have a ghost walking through our house every night."

"He might even bring his friends," Dan said.

"There goes the neighborhood," Kevin said.

"You're just joking because you're scared," Melinda told him.

"I'm not," Kevin said. "I sat right there and watched that ghost walk by me and I didn't even shake."

Dan didn't say anything.

"No, you were too busy clutching me. And you didn't want to open the door to the laundry room," Melinda reminded him. "Your freckles were about to pole-vault over your nose."

"OK. I admit I was scared. But I did it. We've got to get more information if we're going to find out why the ghost is haunting us."

"Maybe it likes you," Dan offered, looking at Melinda.

Melinda glanced at him. Did that mean he liked her? She thought about the ghost and shook her head. "I don't think it even noticed us," Melinda said. "Its attention seemed to be on something ahead of it."

"A ghost with an agenda," Kevin said, snickering.

"That's what we have to find out," Dan said. "What is the ghost's agenda."

6

Melinda shut her eyes tight and gripped the handles of her red racer as she coasted down Holroyd Hill. It was the steepest slope she had ever ridden down. She felt like she was flying. Halfway down she opened her eyes and saw Kevin on his silver racer and Dan on his dark green bike with the rack bolted to the back for carrying papers. At the bottom they crossed Old Manassas Road and got on the bike trail. They were on their way to the library to find out if there had been an old cemetery on Holroyd Hill. Dan had told them about an old map there.

Two blocks from the library they had to leave the trail and ride along the wide leafy street. They locked their helmets to their bikes in the rack at the Broadfalls Library and went inside the red brick building with green shutters.

Dan waved at a blonde woman at the circulation desk. "Hi, Mom." He introduced them to his mother, Suzanne Czernikow. She had green eyes, like Dan's. She was tall and slim. Her hair was a darker blonde than Dan's. She wore a jean skirt and a plaid shirt and long silver earrings. Her smile was a lot like Dan's.

"I'm glad Dan has some company," she said as she shook their hands. "The summer would be lonely for him if you hadn't moved in. Do you have library cards yet?"

They didn't. Mrs. Czernikow gave them the forms to fill out. "I am supposed to have something, a letter addressed to you at that address or something to prove that you live there. But I can vouch for you," she said, handing them the completed cards.

They separated to find books. Melinda grabbed an armload of mysteries. Then she scanned the computer for books about ghosts. Most of them seemed to be fiction but she found a thick one about ghosts in Virginia and checked it out. The boys had a stack of science fiction books.

The enlarged map hung on the back wall. They found Holroyd Hill with Dan's house marked in a tiny square but there was no indication of a cemetery. Kevin was subdued as they unlocked their bikes. He had been sure they would find a cemetery on the map. "It would make things easier in this ghost hunt," he said.

"What do we do now?" Melinda asked.

But Kevin didn't answer. He was quiet on the ride home.

"We'll have to watch the ghost again tonight," Kevin said finally as they walked their bikes up Holroyd Hill.

"Do we have to?" Melinda hadn't planned to see the ghost again. She had decided to avoid the downstairs during the ghost's walk through the house. It was fun to try to solve the mystery of the ghost. It wasn't fun to actually see one. She didn't know why Kevin was suddenly so brave. She glanced at Dan. He made a funny face like he wasn't looking forward to seeing the ghost again, either. She grinned back at him.

"We have to find out all we can," Kevin said, "to stop the ghost from walking."

Kevin was always logical in his own way. Melinda tried one more thing. "Maybe we should tell Mom or Phil."

"No!" Kevin overruled her and Dan agreed.

"But you don't have to watch if you don't want to," Kevin added.

Melinda tossed her head. She wasn't going to be left out. "No way. You're not the Hardy Boys. You don't get to do this without me. I found the ghost, remember. You wouldn't even know about it if I hadn't told you."

"Yes, I would." Kevin grinned. "You don't think you could keep a ghost to yourself all summer? Anyway I would have gone down to the kitchen sooner or later and seen him. Mom and Phil will, too, eventually, so we've got to solve the mystery before they do."

Melinda wondered what would happen if Mom ran into the ghost. She would probably want to represent it in court. And Phil would probably want to sculpt it.

"So we'll all watch again tonight," Kevin said when they reached Dan's mailbox.

"I'll ask my mom." Dan split to go home.

Now that she knew it was there, Melinda could see the roofline of Dan's house through the trees. Just under the eaves a window jutted out on the side facing their house. Somebody could look out that window and see their house, maybe even their backyard. Somebody could watch them. Somebody like Dan's grandfather.

Melinda thought she could feel his eyes on her right now through the trees, those angry eyes watching her. Then she shook herself. She was being silly. Dan's grandfather had better things to do than spy on her. He had his orchards to take care of. But she bet somebody was looking out of that high window.

Dan came over later to report that his mother said he couldn't sleep over two nights in a row. "She thinks your mom will think I've moved in."

"But we won't be able to carry out our plan," Melinda said. "We can't do it without you. You have to come."

"No problem. I can slip out. Mom goes to bed early. Roy stays up watching ball games and old movies in his room. He'll never know I'm gone and he won't mind if he does."

They arranged for Dan to come over after his mom went to her room. Phil watched a baseball game on the TV downstairs while Mom worked late in her office. Melinda read about ghosts in Virginia, but one ear was tuned into the game and the other to her mother's office computer. She hoped Mom would go to bed before 11:30.

" . . . high over center field . . ." The announcer's voice was drowned by the roaring crowd. Melinda was afraid the game would go into a tenth inning but at 11:20 Phil came upstairs in disgust because the Braves had lost by one run. He stopped in the hall and yawned loudly. "Are you going to work much longer?" he asked.

"No," Mom replied. "I'm saving now. I can print in the morning." In a minute she went in Kev's room and then came in and sat on Melinda's bed. "What are you reading?"

Melinda showed her the title.

"That sounds like fun. I always liked ghost stories. The scariest one I ever read was Dorothy Macardle's *The Uninvited*. When the good ghost appeared, there was a warm, friendly aura. When the evil ghost appeared, the aura was cold and frightening. Nobody was home while I was reading it one afternoon. I got so scared I had to run out of the house." She laughed. "I guess I thought a ghost wouldn't follow me outside. I didn't go in until my mother came home from the grocery and asked me what I was doing out in the rain. Luckily it was a warm summer shower."

"I'll look for it in the library," Melinda said. "But I'll only read it when everybody is home."

"You can tell me about Virginia ghosts." Mom sighed. "I don't have time to read for pleasure anymore. Just briefs and research documents."

She kissed Melinda good night. The minute the bedroom door closed, Melinda leaped out of bed. Dan was already at the kitchen door when Melinda opened it to let him in.

"Hurry," she whispered. "He'll be here any minute if he's on time."

Kevin was right behind her, giving orders. "I'll wait in the kitchen," he said. "Dan, you take your position in the breakfast room and Melinda in the family room."

Melinda slowly went through the breakfast area to the family room. She wasn't in a hurry. She didn't want to be alone in the room with the ghost. That was where it had come from the night before. She didn't know how it got there, if it rose out of the floor or came down through the ceiling or out of the fireplace or through the wall or worse, out of the TV. "Oh, creeps," she whispered. "Not the TV."

But the other rooms were scary, too. Any room was scary with a ghost walking through it. Melinda wished she were in the breakfast area with Dan. She would feel safer with somebody.

Melinda's palms began to sweat as she waited for the ghost to appear. She tried to memorize the shapes of the furniture, the fireplace with the painting of kites Phil had done in art school hanging over it, Phil's photographs of old Roman and Greek statues framed and hung on the opposite wall. The house creaked and popped as it cooled for the night. Melinda jumped at every tiny noise.

As she stared at the rectangles of the frames, a light appeared in the middle of Michelangelo's *David* and then the hand holding the light came out of the wall between two of the pictures. Melinda stifled a scream as the body appeared through the wall, first the head, then the legs, then the torso, moving slowly, so slowly.

She looked at the floor in front of her. She couldn't look straight at the ghost, at its face. She might see those ghost eyes looking at her. She clamped her teeth together to keep them from chattering, hoping the ghost wouldn't notice her. She didn't know what it would do. Jump in her face and go "whoo whoo." Attack her. Turn her to stone. She didn't think the ghost would have to do anything. She would probably die of fright if she even caught a glimpse of its face. As the ghost came closer, Melinda shut her eyes and awaited her fate.

But the ghost glided past her as though she wasn't there. She heard the soft shuffling sounds and felt that it had passed her, but there was no breeze from his passage, no little riff of moved air. Her heart was beating like she had just run the Marine Corps Marathon, as the ghost moved slowly into the passage to the breakfast area.

Melinda followed but at a distance. She saw Dan rigid behind the table, his hands holding its edge as he watched the ghost moving steadily forward.

Dan grabbed her arm as the ghost reached the doorway to the kitchen. Melinda squeezed his hand. It was warm and human. It was alive. They moved to the kitchen. Kevin stood in the middle of the far wall right where the ghost had disappeared the night before.

Melinda tried to cry out a warning but she couldn't get any words to come out. In the light from the ghost's lantern she could see Kevin clearly. His face was so white it almost glowed in the lantern light. He looked like he was going to faint but his feet seemed glued to the floor as the ghost bore down on him.

7

*D*an came to life. He grabbed Kevin's arm and pulled him to one side a second before the ghost would have gone through the middle of Kevin. The ghost disappeared through the wall.

Melinda found her voice. "Are you crazy?" she almost shouted. Kevin looked dazed. "What were you trying to do?"

Dan switched on the lights.

"It seemed like a good idea," Kevin said. "I thought if I blocked his way, I might find out something."

"The ghost would have walked right through you," Dan said. "What did you think you would find out?"

"I don't know," Kevin croaked. His voice sounded like he wished he were safely in bed under the covers with the pillows over his head. "What happens when a ghost walks through you?"

"You probably turn into a ghost," Dan said.

Kevin shuddered.

Melinda's back tingled as though a troop of mice were running down it. She was annoyed with Kevin. "Now we've missed our chance to find out where the ghost goes from here," she told him, "all because of you. We're right back where we were last night."

"Not quite." Kevin recovered quickly. "Let's track him down."

They checked the laundry room but it was dark and empty. "He could be in the garage," Melinda said.

"Outside," Kevin said. "The ghost goes outside. Quick."

They went outside the kitchen door just in time to see the lantern disappearing around a bend in the old track through the woods and then the light was swallowed up in darkness.

"Where does he go from here?" Kevin said. "That's what we have to find out."

"That's not all we have to find out," Melinda said.

"What do you mean?"

"Well, if we find out where he goes, we may find some clues, but what we really have to find out is why he is walking. Then we have to help him, so he will stop walking."

The boys looked at her like she was nuts.

"That's what I found out reading about ghosts in Virginia," she explained. "Ghosts only walk to right a wrong that was done to them in life or a wrong that they did themselves. Except for evil ghosts, that is, and I don't think our ghost is evil. Our kind of ghost can't rest until something is done about whatever happened."

"Great," Kevin said. "All we have to do is psychoanalyze a ghost and he will stop walking through our house every night at midnight."

"Don't be silly," Melinda said. "We just have to find out why he is walking. We don't need any of that psychoanalysis stuff."

"Excuse me, Mr. Ghost, but did you kill your wife?" Kevin snickered.

"Or your psychoanalyst?" Dan added.

"No," Melinda said slowly, ignoring their giggles. "I don't think he killed anybody. I think he was the one who was murdered."

The boys stopped laughing.

"Why do you think that?" Dan asked.

"I don't know." The night air suddenly felt almost cold. "I just have this feeling."

"Feelings aren't facts. We have to have more information," Kevin said.

"Just the facts, M'am," Dan said.

"Where do we get facts about a ghost?" Melinda asked.

Dan shrugged.

Not even Kevin had any answers.

"Who knows anything about ghosts?" he said.

The noise of the night crickets suddenly stopped. The silence seemed louder than their clacking and chirping had been. It was the loneliest sound Melinda had ever heard. Nobody seemed to want to speak. Melinda didn't think she could bear that soundlessness, as though the ghost had silenced the entire woods. It seemed to last for hours, but it had probably only been a few seconds before the crickets started up again.

"I'd better go home," Dan said. "I'll come over tomorrow after I deliver my papers. Maybe we can find more data."

....

RAJ was sleeping against the front door when something hit it with a loud thup. He jumped up and growled at the door.

"It's only the paper, you silly dog," Melinda said. But Raj had to prove he was protecting her, so he barked ferociously as she opened the door and picked up the folded edition of the *Broadfalls Gazette*. She checked outside but Dan had already disappeared.

"You can stop barking. See." She held the paper out to Raj, who sniffed it, then wagged his tail when he recognized Dan's scent.

Melinda sat on the bottom stairstep and thumbed through the paper. It had two sections, in addition to the sports section. She looked at the comics first. Some were the same as those in the morning *Post*. Ann Landers and Heloise's columns were the same, too. She looked at some pictures of brides, an Eagle Scout, a church choir embarking on a trip to Salzburg, a gardening column ("How to Pinch Your Impatiens for Their Own Good and Your Visual Delight"). An article on a book caught her eye. *"Broadfalls' First Four Centuries* by Lillian Makepeace is donated by the author to the Broadfalls Library. It tells the story of the town from its birth as a trading post in the seventeenth century to the close of the twentieth century. Ms. Makepeace, descendent of George Luther Makepeace, an eighteenth-century citizen of the town, has written a lively account. 'I tried to make it like a family history,' said Ms. Makepeace. 'I've included all the stories my family handed down and as many as I could track down from other families.' Ms. Makepeace has succeeded admirably. The book is a delight to read. Everyone in Broadfalls will want to own a copy. The book is available at the Broadfalls' Book Nook."

"Kev! Kev!" Melinda yelled.

"Out here," he yelled back from the deck.

He and Dan were working on a box of chocolate chip cookies and sodas. "Hi," Dan said. "I brought my own refreshments today. Have some." He popped the top on a cream soda and pushed the box of cookies toward her as she sat down in one of the chairs.

Melinda munched a cookie as she folded the paper back to show the article to the boys. "We need this book," she said as they finished reading.

"I'll call my mom," Dan said. "She gets books for me sometimes before they go on the shelf at the library. Maybe she can get it for us."

"Call her now," Melinda said. "The phone is in the kitchen."

Dan emerged a few minutes later. "She'll bring it home. I had to convince her we only wanted it to check some stories we've heard. She says the book isn't very well written. It skips around a lot and doesn't have an index."

"What time does she get home?" Melinda asked.

"Five. Sometimes she works the late shift but not tonight."

They only had an hour to wait but it seemed more like ten hours to Melinda. Kevin and Dan went off to Dan's house. They promised to bring the book over as soon as Mrs. Czernikow got home. Kevin didn't seem worried about running into Roy. But he hadn't written that letter. Roy had probably forgotten him and maybe would have forgotten her if she hadn't been so determined to stand up for her rights.

"Come with us," Dan invited.

But Melinda didn't want to chance meeting his grandfather. If he'd forgotten her, she wanted to stay forgotten. She sat on the deck with Raj, who brought her his green tennis ball to throw for him, and tried not to think about the ghost. But she failed. It was impossible not to think about him. Melinda didn't think he meant them any harm. There was no cold aura like Mom had told her about that surrounded evil ghosts. He didn't seem to know they were there. But still—a ghost in their house.

Phil wandered up from his cellar studio to wash some lettuce for dinner and chop some vegetables. Melinda was glad it was his night to cook. He was great at it, chopping vegetables neatly, taking plenty of time, unlike Mom. He came out on the deck and ate a cookie. He was wearing a red T-shirt with "Support your local earthworms" on it. His dark hair was dusted with marble chips.

"You look like you've been in a snowstorm," Melinda said. "Your hair has snowflakes all over it."

"Or dandruff." Phil shook his head. The chips fell on the deck with tiny clinking sounds.

"Pretty hard dandruff."

Phil grinned. "Did the boys go off and leave you again?"

"Not exactly. Dan's mom is bringing home a book we all want to see from the library."

"It must be some book for all three of you to want it," he said.

"It's the one in the paper," Melinda explained.

"Oh, did the paper come?" Melinda handed it to him and he wandered back to the cellar reading as he walked.

....

"MOM was late," Dan explained when he and Kevin returned. "She had to stop at the store."

Kevin took charge of the book and read aloud, "Broadfalls was established in 1691 by a fur trader who bought pelts from the Indians in exchange for knives, beads, and cloth. The trader's name is lost in the mists of time but the little community that grew up there was called Broadfalls in honor of the nearby broadfalls of the Mopotnick River."

"Come on, Kev, I don't think our ghost is an Indian with furs to sell." Melinda reached for the book, but Kevin moved it away and flipped through the pages.

"What are you looking for?" Dan asked but Kevin went on reading.

"Let us have a turn," Melinda said.

"Just a minute. I think I've found something. Look at this." Kevin opened the book flat on the table to a double-page map of Broadfalls 1857. "Holroyd Hill."

Melinda glanced at the map. "It's the same as the map in the library. We've already seen that."

"Yes, we have. But we only looked at it to see if there was an old graveyard under our house. We didn't notice the old road."

"The old road!" Dan exclaimed.

"Look. The road branches off from the Old Manassas Road, comes up Holroyd Hill, swerves around Dan's house, and comes through where our house is and then it stops at the edge of the map." Kevin traced the curves with his finger.

"Of course. That's what the ghost is following," Dan said. "That's why he is haunting your house."

"He doesn't even know our house is there," Kevin said. "He only comes through it because it's built over the road."

"I'll buy that," Dan said.

Melinda thought about it. It made sense. "OK, so he's following an old road. So what? It doesn't tell us anything," she said. "I mean he's only walking through our house because the road runs through it. So we're right back where we started. Maybe even farther back."

"Maybe not. We need to find out where the road went when it reached the end of the map. If we know that, then we might be able to figure out where the ghost is going and why," Kevin told her.

"The map doesn't show where the road goes," Melinda said, studying the pages.

"I know where it goes," Dan said. "It goes down the hill on the other side and connects back to the Old Manassas Road. It makes a loop. The road at the bottom of the hill cuts it off. It goes to Broadfalls the other way."

"So our ghost is coming from Manassas, walking toward Broadfalls," Melinda said.

"We don't know that for sure," Kevin said. "Our ghost is allegedly coming from Manassas."

"We know he wasn't coming from Broadfalls. He's walking *toward* Broadfalls," Dan said.

"He's intent on getting somewhere. It's important enough so that he is walking at midnight alone with only a lantern," Kevin said.

"And maybe with a hurt leg. Maybe his horse fell on him and that's why he is walking," Melinda suggested.

"Supposition," Kevin said.

"I think we have to make some suppositions," Dan said, "or we won't ever be able to solve this mystery."

"It's weird to have a house haunted by a ghost that doesn't even know it's there," Kevin said. "I bet we have the only house in the world that has ever happened to. We could be on TV. Our ghost could be famous."

"Ghosts never show up on those programs," Dan scoffed. "This ghost probably wouldn't either."

"Hey, maybe we should try to film him," Kevin said.

"No." Melinda shook her head. "Nobody believes those pictures and we might scare him away. Whatever the reason, he lets us see him. He's our ghost. It is up to us to find out why and put him at rest. We can't take a chance with cameras."

Melinda knew her thinking was fuzzy. But the ghost seemed so unbearably sad. It was more than just solving a mystery. It was putting right something that happened, something that was wrong a long time ago. Mom always said that justice was necessary for life to go on for people. Maybe it was that way for ghosts, too.

Dan looked at her and nodded. "She's right. I don't know why or what's going on with the ghost, but I think she's right."

"Our ghost is depending on us," Melinda said.

But as she said it, she realized that the ghost was stuck in his own time and didn't even know that they existed.

8

S witch off your flashlight," Kevin said. "Save our batteries."

Melinda flipped the switch at the same time Kevin did and the darkness of the woods seemed to swallow her. "It's spooky," she whispered.

They had decided to wait at the curve of the old road for the ghost to come to them instead of following him through the house and maybe losing him. "We already know what the ghost does in the house. He just walks through it. We need to know what he does outside," Kevin said.

A "star" came toward them through the trees. It seemed almost close enough to touch. The star grew larger and Melinda realized it was Dan. She was glad he was there. Three felt safer to her than two. Frogs were jumping around in her stomach. She wished she hadn't eaten that last taco for dinner.

Something rustled in the bushes. "What was that?" she hissed.

"Maybe a fox. Or a raccoon," Dan said.

Or a bear. Or a snake. Or a ghost. A *ghost*. What were they doing out in the moonless night in the middle of an ancient road waiting for a ghost? Melinda almost laughed aloud. They had seen the ghost inside the house. Now something was about to happen out in the dark of the woods, something different. She wished she were safely tucked into her bed with Raj snuggled up next to her. But they had to solve the ghost's problem.

Melinda was convinced that whatever reason the ghost was walking, it had nothing to do with them. He did not mean them harm, she was sure of that. He didn't even know they were there. He didn't know the house was there or the furniture or anything. He walked only in his own time and only knew what had been there then. She wasn't afraid of him now. She felt badly for him, that something so awful had happened in his life that he had to make that desperate agonizing walk. But if you have one ghost, others could come, sort of like birds at a feeder, she thought.

Raj lay down at her feet and rolled over for her to scratch his stomach.

"Not now, Raj," she whispered.

"Hold his collar," Kevin said. "You shouldn't have insisted on bringing him. We don't want him to jump at the ghost and scare him away."

Melinda didn't think there was any danger of that. Raj was more likely to run away. The first day in the new house he had run away from the new garden hose coiled up under the deck. He'd probably thought it was a snake or a giant worm or some plastic monster. She held his collar with one hand but she put her other arm around him and hugged him tightly. His warm furry bulk felt solid and comforting. He nuzzled her ear as they sat in the grass. Melinda tried not to think what could be crawling around in that grass when Dan said, "He's coming!"

Melinda jumped up, both hands on Raj's collar, her eyes fastened on the edge of the old road. She still had not seen the ghost face-to-face. She had only seen him from the back when she followed him, and the side, and not much of that, when she had been under the table. She thought if she looked in his face she would be haunted by ghost eyes forever. She was glad he was unaware of their presence. She didn't know what she would do if he noticed her or looked straight at her with his ghost eyes.

A light glimmered around the bend in the road and she could hear the faint shuffle of the ghost's feet.

And then he came toward them and her worst nightmare became real. The ghost looked straight at Melinda. His eyes were dark and hooded and did not leave her face. Melinda felt herself shaking as she held onto Raj's collar. Raj whimpered and flattened himself in the weeds as the ghost came closer and closer. She wanted to look away but she couldn't.

Now Melinda saw his face clearly in the light from the flickering lantern. The jaw was clamped tightly, the lips thin and pale. She could see the bulge of muscles on his cheeks. He seemed to be in pain, as though only determination were keeping him going. Melinda didn't know if she actually saw this or if somehow the ghost communicated it to her. But she clearly saw the dark eyes and the dark hair. And this time she saw the letters U.S. clearly on his uniform belt.

The ghost stopped in front of Melinda. If she had reached out her hand she could have touched him. But Melinda couldn't move. She was rooted to the spot, aware only of the dark woods around her, the ghost in front of her and her fingers on Raj's collar.

The ghost stared into her eyes and suddenly there was a look of beseeching anguish in his dark eyes, as though he desperately needed something and she knew that he saw her, that their times had suddenly come together in some kind of focus. The ghost opened his mouth as if to cry out. A burning coldness swept over Melinda and then the ghost moved to her left and vanished.

The cold vibrated around Melinda, a cold that seemed to freeze the air in her lungs and just when she thought she would suffocate from lack of air, the cold was gone and the night was warm again. She stood still. She didn't think she would ever be able to move. And then Dan said, "Wow," and Kevin said, "Did you see that?"

"Did you feel that cold?"

"Yeah," Dan said. "This is supposed to be July. I thought it was January for a minute."

"Maybe it's going to rain," Kevin suggested.

"Nope. Too many stars," Dan said, looking up.

Kevin shrugged. "It could have been a downdraft or something."

"Yeah," Dan agreed, "or something."

"It's connected with our ghost," Melinda said. She was puzzled. They hadn't felt the cold before in the house. Maybe it was because the ghost had looked straight at her. Maybe that was what happened when you looked into ghost eyes. It felt like she imagined falling into a deep dark well would be like with icy black water at the bottom.

Kevin switched on his flashlight and aimed at the bushes. They were still. He shrugged again. "Let's report. What did you see?"

"He was a soldier," Melinda said. "I saw the U.S. on his belt."

"Yeah. I saw it, too," Dan said.

"Those could be his initials, like Ulysses Samuel or something," Kevin argued.

"His clothes looked like a uniform," Dan said.

"OK, I thought so, too. But where did he go?" Kevin probed the thicket with his flashlight beam. Dan turned his on, too, but the beams only lit briers and vines and trees.

Melinda swallowed. "Make an X over there." She gestured to her left where the ghost had disappeared. "And let's come back in the daylight." She didn't know why she was still scared. She had the feeling that the cold was still waiting there somehow, watching them.

Dan found two big sticks and made an X in the leaves.

"There's nothing to see in the dark now anyway," Kevin said.

Melinda could tell that he was a little scared, too. His voice had that little squeak at the end. He kept clearing his throat to hide it. They hurried back down the old road.

Dan left them just past the curve. Melinda realized that this was the little lane drawn on the 1857 map. As she followed Kevin to the house, something seemed to touch her back, between her shoulder blades, and she was sure that someone was looking at her through the thick trees around Dan's house. She was afraid to look back, afraid of what she might see. The night seemed filled with furtive watching eyes.

9

*I*t had probably been Roy watching through the window, she decided the next morning. Her night fears seemed silly with sunlight streaming through the trees, birds singing, the ringing of Phil's chisel like a soprano cricket in the basement. She yawned as she waited for the boys to finish their breakfasts. She had stayed up late reading Ms. Makepeace's book about Broadfalls.

"We're going to search until we find what we're looking for," Kevin declared as he stacked the dishes and took them to the kitchen.

"What's that?" Dan asked.

"Clues," Melinda said as Kevin reappeared with two jugs. She had on her oldest jeans and an old, long-sleeved, red plaid shirt of her mother's. She wasn't taking any chances with poison ivy and briers. Kevin and Dan were dressed for the bush, too. Kevin wore an old pith helmet of Phil's. Melinda and Dan both wore ball caps. Melinda's said Royal Tenaga Yacht Club.

She wore it backwards. Dan's said Cecil's Service Station and shaded his eyes.

"Mush," Kevin said, leading the way.

They stashed the jugs of ice water in a shady spot along the old road. Each carried a long stick to poke the bushes with.

"I wish we knew what clues we were looking for," Melinda said as she examined the ground around the X. "No scorchmarks here. No footprints." She hadn't expected those, but she thought they would find something, some physical evidence of the ghost's passage and disappearance.

"It's simple," Kevin said. "We're looking for what made the ghost vanish last night."

"Ghosts just do that sometimes, don't they?" Dan offered. "I mean, they don't have to have a reason, do they?"

"I think so," Melinda said. "According to the books I've read. They have a reason for doing everything they do."

"Maybe it was another ghost," Dan said.

"They had a ghost duel over a fair damsel," Kevin said dramatically.

Kevin was being silly again. This was serious. "You can joke about it, but something terrible happened to our ghost," she told him.

"Our ghost?" Kevin cocked his eyebrow.

"Well, who else's ghost is he? We're the only ones who have ever seen him."

"How do you know that?" Kevin asked.

"He's not mentioned in that book about Virginia ghosts. So nobody has ever heard of him. I went all through Lillian Makepeace's book last night and didn't find anything about Holroyd Hill in her chapter on visitors from the past. Therefore," she gave Kevin a triumphant look, "nobody has ever seen him before. He's our own private ghost."

Dan poked the bushes with a stick. "There's something strange about him."

"Yeah, right," Kevin said. "He's a ghost."

"No. There's something about him that's not right. Did you see the look on his face?" Dan asked.

"He looked just like a ghost to me," Kevin said. "You've seen one ghost, you've seen them all."

Melinda decided that Kevin was more bothered by this ghost business than he wanted them to know. That must be why he was making all these jokes.

"No," Dan went on. "I had the feeling that something awful was bothering him."

"Me, too," Melinda said slowly. "And I think he was hurt. He looked like he was gritting his teeth. And he walked funny. Kind of lurched. If his leg really was hurt that would explain why he moves so slowly."

"I agree," Dan said.

"If we knew where he was going, it would help a lot," Melinda said.

"Maybe we need to know where he has been," Dan said. "The way he was headed, he could have come from Manassas."

"So?" Kevin beat at a poison ivy vine with a stick.

"He could have been coming from the battle there."

"The Battle of Manassas?" Kevin asked. "The Civil War battle?"

"That's right. It was the first big battle of the Civil War. All the people from Washington went to watch," Dan said.

Kevin stopped beating the bushes. "They went to watch a battle? Like it was a track meet or something?" he asked.

"They even took picnic lunches. Nobody expected it to last more than a few hours. The Union army would whip the Confederates and the war would be over." Dan pushed aside a thorny bush with his stick.

"What happened?" Melinda asked. "I mean, I know it didn't happen that way."

"The Union army panicked about the middle of the afternoon and ran all over the place. The picnickers panicked, too, and tried to get away. Their carriages clogged the roads." He shrugged as if embarrassed to be caught interested in history. "I had to write a report on it in school last year."

Now Melinda knew why their ghost limped. "Our ghost was there," she said.

"How do you know that?" Kevin asked. "You don't have any evidence. You have to have evidence."

"I just know," Melinda said. "He was a Union soldier and he was coming here after the battle."

"Dan just said the battle was over in the afternoon. Our soldier walks by here at midnight. Why did it take him so long?" Kevin argued.

"He was wounded, probably in his leg," Melinda said with certainty. "That's why he drags his foot."

"That would explain why it took him so long to get here after the battle," Dan said. "On foot it would take at least that long walking slowly."

"We don't know that he was in that battle," Kevin objected.

"All right, counselor," Melinda snapped, "we don't know. We don't know anything but what we saw and our feelings. Dan and I think that something is wrong with the ghost. We think he was a soldier. He looked like he was wearing a uniform. There was a U.S. on the belt. I saw it. Dan saw it.

Sometimes you just have to put things together and go on."

"What if you're wrong?" Kevin said.

"Then if we prove we're wrong, we'll try something else."

"Let's try to find out why the ghost disappears at this spot every night," Dan said. "Keep looking for clues." He lifted a tangle of Virginia creeper with his stick.

"What if you don't find anything?" Kevin persisted.

"You're impossible, Kevin." Melinda stomped away from the X, the spot where the ghost had left the road before vanishing. The cold didn't seem to be there in the solid heat of the morning. Maybe it had been imagination or nerves the night before. She moved in a straight line out from the X, studying the ground for clues. Whatever made the ghost vanish had to be around here.

The brush thickened but she kept going. To her left she could see Dan doing the same thing. Noises on her right suggested that Kevin was looking, too.

Melinda wished she had worn gloves as she parted a tangle of briers in front of her face and ducked under a loop of poison ivy vine with a stem almost as thick as her wrist. She stopped to unsnag her hair from a low limb and tried to stuff it under her hat. Her hair looked like copper in the sun but it wasn't as bright as Kevin's. When a brier swiped at her eyes, she turned her hat around so the bill would protect them.

Kevin whacked the bushes. "See, there's nothing here," he said.

Melinda half-turned to retort in midstep and suddenly the ground was no longer under her feet.

"Help!" she yelled as she tumbled downward.

She came to a stop on a pile of stones covered with briers and matted leaves. It was the same place she had fallen the day they went exploring and met Roy Sasser. She dug around in the leaves and found more gray rocks with bands and streaks of marble. Cold air seemed to hover around the edge of the depression.

"That's it!" she shouted. "I've found it!"

Dan and Kevin scrambled down to her.

"What? What have you found? I don't see anything," Kevin added.

"Are you OK?" Dan asked.

"Yeah. Remember, Kev, the other day when we met—um—Dan's grandfather?"

"I remember. So what's that got to do with this?"

"I got lost when we were exploring," she explained to Dan. "I fell down in here and found these rocks. I took one home."

"Yeah. So?" Kevin said.

"That night I saw the ghost."

"What's that got to do with anything?"

"I get it," Dan said. "You think the rock had something to do with making the ghost appear."

"It's the only thing that fits. I mean this is near the spot where the ghost disappears," Melinda said excitedly.

"What's that got to do with a pile of rocks?" Kevin asked.

"Maybe nothing," Melinda said. "Maybe it's what's under the pile of rocks."

The woods were suddenly silent. Melinda felt her pulse pounding. She jumped to her feet as though the gray stones were hot lava rocks. She could see that the boys were thinking the same thing she was.

"We need shovels," Dan said.

"Somebody should stay here," Kevin said.

Melinda looked at Dan. "No way," they said together.

They separated on the road and returned shortly with shovels. Dan had brought a pair of Roy's shears to cut a path down to the rocks so the going was easier this time.

"Let's clear the rocks away first," Dan said.

They threw the rocks into a pile about six feet away. The gray rocks were as cold as ice. Probably because the sun didn't penetrate the thicket above, Melinda thought. She cradled one in her hand but instead of warming it with the heat of her hand, the rock seemed to grow colder. She threw it into the pile and flexed her fingers to warm them.

Then Dan picked up his shovel. He pushed it into the ground with his foot. Kevin picked up his shovel. Melinda scooped up a shovelful of dirt.

The ground was soft and easy to dig, despite the cold that seemed to come and go. Now it was hot in the low, bowl-shaped place.

"We're below the breezes," Kevin said, wiping the sweat off his face with the back of his hand.

"I think we're in a sinkhole," Dan said, leaning on his shovel.

"What's a sinkhole?" Melinda kept digging.

"Where the ground sort of collapses because it gets too heavy for the limestone underneath. See how smooth the sides are. We have one in the back of the orchard."

"Will it sink any more with us in it?" Kevin asked.

"Probably not. It probably happened a long time ago."

"Maybe over a hundred and fifty years ago," Melinda said dreamily. "Before the Civil War."

"And then what?" Kevin said.

"Maybe—oh! What's that?" Her shovel clinked against something. But it was only a small rock.

They stopped for a water break. Nobody wanted to speculate about what they might find. It might be nothing, Melinda thought to herself. But she didn't believe it. The place where the ghost disappeared had to be important.

She felt refreshed after the water and dug with renewed energy. Her shovel hit something solid. She scraped at the dirt with the edge of the shovel. This time it wasn't a rock. It was a piece of metal, sort of oval shaped and rusted.

"Look! I found something."

Kevin and Dan crowded closer.

"What is it?"

"I don't know."

"Pick it up," Kevin said.

Melinda reached downward, then drew her hand up. "No, I—look, shouldn't we be doing this with trowels or something like archaeologists do?"

"You're right," Kevin said. "I'll go get some. You two stay here and keep digging with the shovels but carefully."

"Is he always that bossy?" Dan asked.

"Most of the time. Mom says he'll make a great lawyer. Lawyers think they know everything."

Dan laughed and lifted out half a shovelful of the red clay dirt that underlay the woods' humus. There was something in it. Melinda pointed. "I see it," he said.

"It looks like a bone. But it could be a rock."

"No, I think it's a bone." He picked it up. "It looks like a knucklebone."

"It could be a raccoon's," Melinda said.

"It could be, but I don't think it is. I think a raccoon's would be smaller." His voice sounded worried. He looked at Melinda. "Are you thinking what I'm thinking?"

Melinda nodded and went on digging. Kevin came back with

two trowels, a digging fork, a large kitchen spoon, plastic bags, notebook, pen, and a cardboard box.

"We have to do this scientifically," he said.

Melinda looked at Dan. "No."

"What do you mean no?" Kevin pulled on a pair of his mother's flowered garden gloves.

"I mean—" and she stopped. What she was about to say was too weird. "I mean this is a ghost, not a science project. He was a person. I don't want to put him in little bags. Let's just put what we find altogether in the box. OK?"

Melinda didn't think her words quite made sense, but Dan understood. He nodded. "Yeah."

"OK. OK. I don't know what difference it makes between a box or a plastic bag. Let's just get to the bottom of this . . ." Kev looked at them.

"Grave," Dan finished his sentence and looked at Melinda.

She stared back at him. So he thought the same thing. But she kept quiet. They didn't have the evidence to satisfy Kevin.

"Let's dig, guys," Kevin ordered.

They dug in silence until Kevin uncovered the rib cage and almost fainted. They threw water in his face.

"It's bones, it's really bones, somebody's ribs," he moaned.

"Kevin, you're babbling," Melinda said.

"I mean, it could be a cow's rib cage, couldn't it?" he said.

"Sure it could," Melinda said. But she could tell by his face that he didn't believe her.

They returned to their digging, the boys working carefully around the curved rib bones. Melinda worried about the cold. It seemed to be watching from the rim of the sinkhole, waiting as though it had eyes, a brain, hands, talons. She tried to work faster so they could get out of the sinkhole.

She reached for a large rounded rock like the cobblestones found all over the area. She picked it up to throw it into the pile with the others. But the rock was light, too light for a cobblestone with the red clay stuck to it. Melinda scraped the rock with a stick and turned it over. It had the markings of a face, two holes for the eyes, a hole for the nose, a large one for a mouth all filled with red clay. Melinda sat cross-legged, staring at it for a long time. She had picked up a lot of rocks in her collecting. But she had never found a rock like this. It felt alive and dead at the same time. And she knew it was not a rock. At last she said in a low voice, "Dan. Kevin."

Dan noticed first. His breath went out with a kind of hiss like air out of a tire. "Oh, no. Oh, no."

"Oh, no, what?" Kevin turned around. He saw the rock in Melinda's lap.

"It's a skull." He didn't faint this time. The three sat quietly staring at the skull. Finally Kevin said, "Get it out of your lap."

"I'm not afraid of it," Melinda said. "It's his. He doesn't mean me any harm."

"That doesn't have anything to do with it," Kevin said. "How can you sit there calmly with that thing in your lap?"

"I don't know. I just can." But she lifted it gingerly and placed it in the box.

There was no longer any doubt about the rib cage now. It was definitely human. They used sticks and twigs to brush the dirt away from the bones. They found other bones, long ones from arms and legs and small ones they didn't recognize. They found rusted brass buttons and a rusted metal U.S. and several small disks they thought were coins. Dan found what looked like a pocket watch. On the back they could just make out the initials D.C. Inside it they found something soft and bright.

"It looks like hair," Dan said.

"It might have been from his girlfriend," Melinda suggested. "People used to do that. It could be his mother's or his sister's," she added. But she was sure the hair had belonged to his girlfriend.

"Let's put this stuff in the box," Kevin said. He had recovered and taken charge again. But as they lifted the rib cage, Melinda saw a lump of something in the middle where it had lain in the dirt.

And then the cold struck.

10

*W*e've got to get out of here," Kevin said through chattering teeth.

"No," Melinda and Dan said together.

"We've got to finish," Dan said.

"But what ab-bout the c-cold?" Kevin said.

"Something is trying to drive us away," Dan said. "Try to ignore it."

It was like wearing a coat of ice. Melinda thought she could stand it as long as nothing actually touched her. Like a hand or—she pushed those thoughts aside and concentrated on the small lump of clay she plucked out of the ground. But her fingers slowed as the cold solidified around her. It seemed to be sucking away her warmth. The lump was heavy, heavier than a lump of clay should be and heavier than most rocks of that size. Melinda scraped at the lump. Her fingers were clumsy but she refused to stop.

"I won't let it stop me," she repeated to herself over and over.

Gradually the cold began to ease.

"It's l-leaving," Kevin said. "The power of m-mind over m-matter."

The cold went away as quickly as it had come.

"It's the ghost," Kevin said. "Ghosts have a cold aura."

"No, only bad ghosts," Melinda said, "I'm sure it's not our ghost. I've never felt cold when he walks through the house."

"Then it must have something to do with the sinkhole," Kevin decided.

Melinda tapped the lump with her trowel. There was a metallic ting.

"Look," she said, almost whispering. "I think it's a bullet."

Dan picked it up. He wiped it on his jeans. "It is a bullet. A lead bullet. I've seen lots of them in antique stores, jars of them. They cost a dollar. They're Civil War bullets. See the grooves in the end?"

"Where did it come from?" Kevin asked. Melinda knew where it came from even as Dan replied, "It was inside his chest."

She felt a sudden aching somewhere inside her own rib cage, somewhere near her heart.

"He couldn't have walked here all the way from Manassas with that in him," Dan said in a low voice.

"Are you guys thinking what I'm thinking?" Kevin asked.

"Somebody killed him here and buried him at the side of the road," Melinda said. "That's why he was walking. He wanted someone to know, to find him where he's been for all these years alone in the woods . . ." Her voice trailed off. It was so sad. "His family never knew what happened to him. Nobody knew but the person who buried him, maybe the same person who killed him."

"But who?" Dan said.

"And why," Melinda added.

"Another soldier probably followed him from the battle and killed him," Kevin said. "A Confederate soldier."

"The Confederates didn't pursue," Dan said. "That was one of their major mistakes. They could have taken Washington and history would have been a lot different."

"They didn't pursue into Washington. They could have followed some of the soldiers this far," Kevin insisted.

"I don't think so. The Union army was camped all around here," Dan said. "There was even a camp on the other side of Holroyd Hill."

"Maybe that's where he was going," Melinda said.

Dan shook his head. "No, he would already have passed it in the direction he takes every night."

Kevin put the bullet in a bag in the box. "If he was murdered here, that would explain the cold, I guess."

Nobody said anything.

They dug up pieces of what they thought were boots, bits of fabric, buttons. Kevin put the personal things in a bag with the bullet.

They dug until there were no more bones to be found in the clay. Melinda looked at the things in the box. Once they had been a man. He'd had a family, friends, a life. They probably never knew what had happened to him. He'd died here on the road and this was all that was left. Something seemed to be missing. Melinda couldn't think what it could be.

"What are we going to do with, um, well, the bones?" Melinda asked.

"We should bury them somewhere," Kevin said. "right away."

"But where?" Dan asked.

"I think we should try to find out what the ghost wants us to do," Melinda said. "I mean, I brought the rock from his grave home with me. I think that is what started him walking. He led us here. We discovered he was killed and left here."

"Maybe that was all he wanted. Maybe he wouldn't mind if we buried him here again," Kevin said.

"Or maybe he doesn't want to be here," Dan said. "That may be the reason he's walking. Whoever buried him hid the grave."

"How do you know that?" Kevin asked. "I mean he could have fallen in the hole."

"The rocks were piled over the bones."

"They could have rolled down the sides of the hole," Kevin said.

"I don't think so, not that many," Dan said. "And they're different from the cobblestones we've found in the woods. I think they were brought here in a load like in a wheelbarrow and dumped."

Kevin was unconvinced. "Suppositions. But we can put him in the garage for now," he said as he picked up the box. "We've solved the mystery. He was leading us to his grave. He won't be walking through our house anymore."

Melinda wasn't so sure. She was glad to leave the sinkhole. She was sure the ghost didn't want to be reburied there. It was a horrible place. Not even a proper grave.

Kevin carried the box back to their garage and put it high on a shelf.

"It will be safe there until we decide what to do. Phil is too busy with his fish to notice and Mom doesn't care what's in the garage. If she found the bones she would probably tell them to pull themselves together and give them her card," Kevin joked.

Melinda's room was over the garage. It made her feel peculiar knowing that the soldier was there underneath her, almost like having her room over a cemetery. She wasn't afraid of the soldier. She felt comfortable with him now. He wasn't a threatening ghost like some she had read about, only greatly troubled and unhappy. And as Kevin had said, he seemed to have an agenda.

But she was afraid of the strange cold at the end of the ghost's path and the cold that came and went around the grave.

And she couldn't stop thinking about the soldier killed after the first battle of the war. His parents somewhere in Indiana maybe or Maine wondered all their lives what happened to him. And maybe his sweetheart or even his wife. Now after all these years, she and the boys had found him. She thought about the bright strands of hair and her thoughts drifted.

....

MELINDA woke from a light sleep that night and glanced at her bedside clock. The time glowed in the dark. 11:30. She had become accustomed to being up at this hour. She put on her sneakers and tiptoed out into the hall and ran into Kevin. He had his flashlight.

"Something woke me up," he whispered.

"Me, too. Do you think it was the soldier?"

"I don't know. I've never known a ghost before."

Melinda hoped they wouldn't see the soldier's bones walking through the house. A ghost wasn't so bad. But a skeleton was unacceptable. They reached the bottom stair just as the lantern light glimmered in the family room as the ghost entered through the wall.

"He's here," she whispered. She closed her eyes, afraid of what she would see. But she couldn't close her ears to the sound of something sliding across the floor. A skeleton wouldn't make that kind of noise, she decided. She opened her eyes to the now-familiar sight of the soldier as he glided across the floor. This time Melinda could see that he was dragging his right leg. He seemed to move even more slowly than before. His face wore the same anguished look, his mouth drawn in a look of intense suffering not entirely from his physical pain, Melinda thought.

The ghost melted through the kitchen wall. Melinda and Kevin slipped out of the kitchen door in time to follow him down the track. He disappeared at the same place as before. Melinda backed away, dragging Kevin with her.

"Let's get out of here before the cold comes," she said.

They raced back to the house.

"I guess we didn't solve his problem," Kevin said at the door.

"I guess not."

They went back to bed but Melinda couldn't sleep from thinking about the look on the soldier's face. Something had happened to him out there that was so terrible he had to keep walking to try to find a solution. It was connected with the terrible cold. But Melinda didn't know how. The ghost couldn't solve what had happened to him in life. Somehow he had chosen her—them—to help him, to be his champions against whatever the cold represented. Like Mom in a courtroom. She'd once explained to Melinda that a lawyer defending a client was like a knight in a tournament. She and Dan and Kevin were the ghost's knights. It was up to them.

....

MELINDA dozed and woke up again. The night was hot. The ceiling fan stirred the curtains, making them look like ghosts. From somewhere inside her she felt something that she couldn't describe. Something outside the window pulled her to it, something calling her, but Melinda heard no voice. She got up and leaned on her windowsill. The air outside was cooler but it was still a warm summer night. In the moonlight she could see the roof of Dan's house. It had been built in 1842, he'd said. That meant it had been here in 1861. The people who lived there would have known what had happened at Manassas that day. Maybe they had even gone to watch the battle, packed a picnic lunch, put on their best clothes, and driven over in their carriage to watch the soldiers killed. They would have surely known about the soldiers at the Union camp down the road. A chill ran down her spine. The people in Dan's house were connected with what happened to the soldier. Melinda was sure of it.

As she stared at the roof Melinda thought she saw something at a window high up under the eaves. It was the same window she'd thought someone was watching her from several times before. But this time the impression seemed clearer, as though someone with an anguished heart was calling from beyond the grave. The answer was there. They just had to find it. But it was hard to look for an answer when you didn't know what the question was.

11

The investigation was stuck. Even Kevin admitted it. The ghost still walked through the house. They tracked it two more nights. It still disappeared on the old road. Finding the bones hadn't changed anything. Except that now they had ghost bones in a box in the garage. Melinda felt uncomfortable about that but she didn't know what they should do about it. They had a meeting on the back deck. Dan brought over a pan of apple muffins still warm from the oven to help them think.

"We can't just let the ghost bones stay in the garage forever," Kevin said. "Phil will be sure to find them. Then we'll really have some explaining to do."

"Well, we're not going to put them back where we found them. The ghost doesn't want us to do that." She thought the ghost seemed more anguished each night but she didn't mention it. Kevin would say it was supposition. She reached for another muffin. "These are great," she told Dan.

"Roy made them."

Melinda almost choked. She went in the kitchen and got a glass of water. She sipped it, while the boys worked on the muffins, and she thought about Roy. He probably hadn't even read her letter. Probably he had put it down somewhere and it got thrown away in the trash.

"We didn't stop the ghost from walking but I think he is either giving up on us or he's wearing out. He looked awfully tired last night," Dan said.

"He did look a little faded," Kevin said. "Less dense. The lantern light didn't look as bright. It seemed dimmer."

"What did you say?" Melinda stared at her brother.

Kevin repeated his sentence.

"That's it!" Melinda said.

"What? What's what?" Kevin asked.

"Something was missing from the box of bones. I couldn't think what it was but now I know."

"The lantern," Dan said.

Melinda nodded. "How did you know?"

"I don't know. I just kept seeing a spot of light."

"What about the lantern?" Kevin asked as he bit into another muffin.

"Don't you see?" Melinda said. "The lantern wasn't in the grave. Mom always says to look for what's not there."

"That's why we didn't miss it because it wasn't there," Dan said. "The lantern is missing."

"The Case of the Missing Lantern," Melinda said.

"That's no mystery," Kevin said. "The murderer probably took it home to his wife and said, 'Honey, look at this nice new lantern I got you.' "

Melinda's excitement plummeted. She hadn't thought of that. She had thought it was a real clue. But a clue to what?

"Wait a minute," she said to Kevin. "You said murderer. I thought you said that the ghost was killed by another soldier."

"Yeah. So?"

"But that's not considered murder. What made you say murderer?"

Kevin glanced around the tree-shaded backyard as if to search for whomever had put the word in his mouth. He scratched his head. His red hair looked like he'd combed it with the food processor. "I don't know. I don't think it was murder. I mean, if a soldier killed another soldier after a battle, that's not considered murder."

"Even if the soldier was wounded?" Melinda said.

"He could have even been shot by another Union soldier," Kevin said. "He could have been considered a deserter, running away from the battlefield."

"They would have had to shoot a lot of soldiers," Dan said. "They probably wouldn't have shot a wounded soldier from their own side for leaving the battlefield."

"It was dark," Kevin insisted.

"But he had a lantern," Melinda reminded him. "At least he had it until he was killed."

They were silent, remembering why the soldier was a ghost. Melinda tried to imagine Holroyd Hill in 1861. Their house wasn't there. Nor was the paved court and street. The old road cut through the thick woods, traveled only by wagons and horsemen and people on foot. They would have passed by Dan's house.

"Does your grandfather ever go anywhere?" she asked Dan.

"Why? You don't think he shot the ghost. He's not old enough. I don't even think my great-grandfather would have been old enough."

"No. But I think the answer is in your house." She told them about the shape in the window.

"You've got ghosts on the brain," Kevin said.

Dan looked at her. "How did you know that?"

"Know what?"

"About the woman in the attic window?"

"I didn't. I mean, I just sort of felt like someone was there watching from the window."

"My mom said Great-aunt Hannah saw a woman in the attic window. She had been visiting for months. The family wanted her to leave. Everybody thought it was Roy playing a trick on her so she'd go. He swore he didn't do it. He was a kid then." Dan reached for another muffin but forgot to take a bite. His hand dropped. Raj ate the muffin out of his hand, then licked his fingers but he didn't even notice. Finally he said, "Roy went to Leesburg to look at a tractor."

A surge of excitement ran through Melinda. This was their chance. "How long do you think he'll be gone?"

"A couple of hours." Dan's green eyes were puzzled.

Melinda explained her thinking. "I think the answer is in Dan's house. I think the soldier was going somewhere and he didn't get there. That's why he walks."

"Supposition," Kevin objected. He scooped up the crumbs from the muffin pan.

"But it fits."

"You can't just make stuff up to fit what you think happened," Kevin persisted.

"We have to prove it, that's all," Melinda said.

"How?" Kevin asked.

"We'll go look around at Dan's house. If that's OK with you," she amended, looking at Dan.

He laughed. "You're almost as bossy as your brother. Let's go look but I don't know what we'll find."

Melinda didn't know either. She just knew they had to look. "I'm not bossy, just determined. There's a difference. You're not the one who is sleeping over a garage with human bones in a box on the shelf."

Dan stopped laughing. "No. You're right. We have to search for every clue. Our house was here at that time. It seems like a logical place to look." He was quiet for a minute. "And then there's the woman in the window."

"You think Dan's ghost knew our ghost?" Kevin asked.

"I don't know. We have to eliminate the obvious." There. Let him argue with that, she thought.

....

DAN's house wasn't like Tara or Mount Vernon or the grand plantation houses of Virginia that Melinda had seen. It was a wooden two-storied house with a third story in the attic. A railed porch held up by plain round posts ran along the front of the house. It was white and needed painting. The porch was furnished with big wooden rockers and a swing at one end. A cloud of purple wisteria hummed with bees at the other end.

Dan opened the screen door and they entered a hall as wide as a room. It was gloomy and hushed after the light and noise outside. Melinda could see glass-fronted bookcases, a hall tree hung with straw hats, a bamboo chair, a whatnot stand in the corner. She hung back, reluctant to enter. She knew Dan's grandfather was supposed to be away. But this was where he lived. If he came home suddenly, he might yell at her to stay away from his house and forbid Dan to see her.

"Come on," Dan said from the stairway at the end of the hall.

The boys went ahead up the winding narrow stairway to the second floor. Melinda followed slowly. It had been her idea but now that she was actually here in the ogre's house, she wished she weren't. She had an uneasy feeling.

The boys were out of sight, already in the attic when she reached the second floor. The air suddenly became cooler. She thought the air conditioner must be on but it was colder than any air conditioning she had ever felt. The light was dim, the stairs so narrow her elbows brushed the walls which were covered in a splotched pale brownish-colored paper. And then she saw him at the top of the stairs, the same pointed white beard, bushy black eyebrows, dark eyes, the same fierce scowl. He wasn't in Leesburg. He was here. He stretched his arm and pointed at her as he came down the stairs toward her, slowly.

Melinda backed down the stairs. She was afraid to turn around, afraid of what he would do when she couldn't see him, but afraid to keep looking at those awful eyes. She had never seen anyone with such mean eyes. Why was she so cold? It must be fear. She was turning to ice. In another minute she wouldn't be able to breathe. She couldn't move. The cold was numbing her.

He loomed over her, closer, closer as he seemed to glide down the stairs toward her, those awful staring eyes coming nearer, nearer. She had to get away. With great effort, Melinda put her left foot behind her and felt her way down the stairs, one foot at a time, slowly, slowly as the cold replaced her energy. She had to hurry before she was frozen solid. But her feet seemed to move so slowly. Her toes were already numb.

He was gaining on her. Melinda felt behind her. Another

step. Another. Those evil eyes seemed to be coming at her ahead of the body, stabbing her with their fierce anger.

"I'm sorry," Melinda stammered. But she wasn't sorry. "I didn't mean to be rude," she corrected herself. "I just wanted you to understand why we wouldn't bother y-your old orchards." Roy Sasser didn't pay any attention to her words. He didn't seem to hear them. He came closer and closer.

Melinda reached the second floor. She almost stumbled with relief. She grabbed the wall to steady herself. It felt like a sheet of ice. She collected her energy and turned. When she could no longer see the man, she was able to move faster. It was as though he had put some kind of spell on her. She ran down the next flight of stairs, gathering speed as the distance between her and Roy Sasser lengthened, down the hall, out the door where she gulped the sun-drenched air as she ran. She didn't stop until she was home on her own deck where she could hear Phil at work and hug Raj.

The boys found her there about ten minutes later.

"Why didn't you tell us you were coming home?" Kevin said. "I thought you were dying to search Dan's attic."

"You said your grandfather wasn't home," Melinda accused Dan.

"He's not."

"Yeah, right. I *saw* him."

"You couldn't have. He's not there."

"He was there. He was on the stairs to the attic. Didn't you see him?"

"No," Kevin said.

"He couldn't have been. There was nobody in the attic when we went up there," Dan said.

"I know what I saw. I saw your grandfather."

"Look, he left in his car. Come over and look for the car. If you find it, then we'll know you saw him. If we don't . . ." Dan let his words trail off.

Melinda shook her head. She never wanted to see Roy Sasser again. Her teeth were still cold. She bet her hair was, too.

"Don't you want to try the attic again?" Dan asked.

"You can look without me."

"No," Dan said. "You're the only one of us who has seen the—our ghost. I think you have to be in the attic with us. I don't think Kevin and I can find anything without you."

Melinda was torn. Dan wanted her to come. She needed to, but she couldn't risk seeing his grandfather. She didn't ever want to go in that house again. She would never forget those eyes.

Melinda made her decision. Give her a ghost any day or night over Dan's grandfather. Dan didn't understand. Roy was, after all, his grandfather. But Melinda knew Kevin did. "Sorry," she mumbled to her feet.

Dan looked at her for a few minutes. "I've gotta go deliver papers," he said and went back through the woods. But he didn't deliver papers until Friday. Now she'd made Dan mad or hurt his feelings, or disgusted him. Or all three.

Kevin went down to the basement to talk to Phil but Melinda didn't feel like talking to anybody. She should have gone back. It was stupid of her. Dan's grandfather couldn't help what he looked like. Well, he could shave his beard or at least cut the point off and smile at people. But the cold—she couldn't explain the cold.

Melinda curled up in her room and read all afternoon with Raj at her feet for protection. She ignored the ghost book and read animal stories. After supper, she read about a girl who ran for class president, a story as far away from ghosts and grandfathers as she could get. One of the characters was antisocial. Melinda looked the word up. Averse to society, the society of people. That's what Dan's grandfather was, antisocial, she thought.

When Mom came in to kiss her good night, she looked at the book title. "Giving up on ghosts?" she asked.

Melinda smiled and kissed her back. Wasn't that exactly what she was doing, giving up on her ghosts? Uncomfortable, Melinda burrowed down into the pillow as Mom turned off the light and went out. The curtains swelled with breeze in her window but she ignored them. She knew if she looked out the window at midnight she would see a light on the old road and a face in the attic window of Dan's house. With each movement of the curtains she felt a sense of urgency.

The image of the sad ghost kept jumping into her eyes and she couldn't shake the nagging feeling that she was letting him down. She was letting Dan down as well. He believed in his grandfather. He couldn't understand why she was afraid of Roy Sasser. But he hadn't had the experience Melinda and Kevin had had. And he hadn't written that letter. If only she hadn't done that. Melinda turned over and thought about the ghost.

She couldn't forget his anguished eyes like deep pools of sadness. And she couldn't forget that he seemed to be fading, as though he were running out of time. Maybe she had imagined Roy and the cold. She had been like her mother rushing out of the house when she was reading that book. Melinda thought she understood that awful cold now. It was terror. She and the boys had been terrified in the sinkhole. And she had been terrified on the stairs. That's all it was. Ordinary everyday terror.

12

Thin black snaky branches pulled at Melinda's shirt as she ran through the woods. She had lost Kevin and Dan. She called but there was no answer. The woods were getting darker. She couldn't see her own hands now. She tried to run faster but her feet wouldn't obey her. Suddenly she saw a pale light through the trees ahead. It had to be the boys. But just as suddenly the light disappeared. Melinda stopped to catch her breath. The sinkhole gaped in front of her. As she leaned over it, Roy Sasser popped up out of it, an evil grin stretching across his face.

Melinda started to scream and woke up. Her room was dark. Her clock showed three A.M. She lay in the dark thinking about what she had to do.

Somewhere around dawn a light rain fell and Melinda went to sleep. The sun was shining when she woke up again. She hoped Dan would be sitting on the deck when she went downstairs. He would be sitting there maybe with some of Roy's muffins and everything would be the same. But it wasn't.

When she looked out the kitchen door she saw Kevin sitting alone at the table.

"Where's Dan?"

Kevin shrugged and kept reading the *Post* comics.

Melinda made toast, spread it with jam, and poured a glass of milk. She slid into the opposite chair and Raj lay down across her bare feet. She'd hoped Dan wouldn't stay mad. Maybe he'd said something to his grandfather and Roy had said, "I don't want you to see those kids anymore."

Great. She had ruined the rest of the summer. He was their only friend. Breakfast suddenly didn't taste so good. Melinda broke her toast up in little pieces and fed them to Raj. He smacked his big loose lips as he took the tiny pieces gently from her fingers. Strawberry jam was his favorite.

She and Kevin needed Dan's help to solve the mystery. She was convinced the answer was in his attic. But she had ruined that, too.

Just as she finished her milk Dan came loping out of the woods. He sat on the edge of the deck and scratched Raj, who rolled over in ecstasy. Without looking at Melinda he said carefully, "My grandfather just left for Dulles Airport to meet a friend who is passing through Washington. He'll be gone for hours if you want to try again."

Melinda knew she had to. She couldn't be stupid again and risk her friendship with Dan. It wasn't Dan's fault Roy was antisocial. She didn't want him to feel bad. And she couldn't let the ghost down again. There was also the time factor. The soldier's light was fading. Who knew what that meant? "All right," she said. "But I'm not going up those stairs last this time."

"All right!" Kevin said. "Let's go now."

They dumped their dishes in the dishwasher without rinsing and raced to Dan's house. Melinda slowed down as they went up the first flight of stairs, ready to bolt at the first sight of Roy. At the attic stairway, Kevin went first, then Melinda, then Dan. Melinda kept looking behind her.

"It's OK," Dan whispered. "There's nobody but me back here."

She reached out and touched the wall. It felt like a wall, not ice.

Once in the attic Melinda thought she was safe. Dan's grandfather wouldn't be hiding there ready to jump out and scare her. He had more important things to do. And if he were antisocial, wouldn't he want to avoid her and Kevin? Now that she was here in the attic, she decided, maybe it had been her imagination the day before.

The attic was divided into two rooms with sloping walls. Both rooms were full of boxes and old furniture, chests, trunks, old suitcases, and stacks of magazines tied into bundles with string. Melinda looked at the top on one pile and read the cover, "*Cosmopolitan*, September 1932, Beginning *Black Sheep, Black Sheep*, Warwick Deeping's New Novel." Not old enough. She had expected to feel something in the attic, a presence, some kind of directional pointer, a sign. But the attic just seemed like a closed-up room, dim, dusty, cobwebby, hot. She didn't know where to start.

The boys opened some of the trunks and chests. Melinda plunged her hands into a chest of clothes. They were old but not old enough. No hoop skirts or ruffled petticoats. She withdrew her hands and smelled them. They smelled musty like the clothes. She sneezed and moved over to the window. She tried to open it but it was painted shut in the frame. It would take a chisel and a lot of work to get it open. She went in the front room and tried that window. Same problem. The glass in the window was wavy. It was like looking through water. She glanced down at the old road below and a portion of the paving of Holroyd Hill Circle. She leaned on her elbow and looked straight out through the trees. The window in her room over the garage was directly in line with this one. If I were home looking out that window I could see myself, she thought illogically. This was the haunted window.

"Hey, quit daydreaming and start looking for clues," Kevin ordered, unstacking boxes in the back corner.

Melinda opened a box of old stuffed animals with missing eyes and ears and limbs but too loved to be thrown away. "Go back to sleep," she whispered to them.

"I don't think your family has ever thrown anything away," Kevin said to Dan as they sifted through a box of broken kitchenware.

"That's why people have attics," Melinda said. "So you don't have to throw things away."

"It looks like it's never been cleaned either," Kevin said.

Dan laughed. "It hasn't. Every few years somebody comes up and dusts a little. Mom says nobody has the energy to clean out all this stuff."

They took a lemonade break in the big sunny kitchen that had been added onto the back of the house. A brick fireplace and rocking chairs promised coziness in the winter. The mantel was crowded with candlesticks, glass lanterns, pottery animals, old bills. A gray cat was asleep in a cushioned rocker. Dan said his name was Mosby, after the gray ghost of the Confederacy. Mosby purred and pushed at Melinda's hand with his head when she stroked his soft fur.

The house seemed as friendly as the cat to Melinda. It smelled good, too, like apples and cinnamon. Tabletops were cluttered with nursery catalogs, newspapers, books, orchard pamphlets, and magazines. It seemed like a place where people lived, a family, not ghosts and not ogres like Dan's grandfather.

A clock bonged the hour. Twelve. If this were at night, we would see the soldier ghost walking, Melinda thought. We could see it from the attic window. Where the ghost is. Suddenly she put all the fragments together. "Your ghost watches our ghost walk toward her along the road."

"What?" Dan and Kevin were both looking at her.

"What did you say?" Kevin asked.

"The ghost in Dan's attic watches our ghost as he walks along the road."

"No, that's not what you said," Kevin told her.

"Yes, it is. I said the ghost watches our ghost as he walks along our road."

"No, you said 'as he walks toward her'."

"Well, so what?"

"I think she's right," Dan said. "Our ghost is supposed to be female. If there are two ghosts in an area this close, there is probably a connection between them."

"Suppo . . ." Kevin began.

" . . . sition," Dan and Melinda finished for him.

"Yeah," Dan said. "We know. But sometimes you have to work on those suppositions."

Kevin didn't seem happy about the idea of another ghost. "I don't believe there's anything in the attic. It's awfully hot and dusty up there. Let's go to our house and go through our notes."

Melinda was sure the answer was in the attic. They didn't

need to go back over their notes or make any new ones. Sometimes Kevin was too lawyerly. But she wasn't sorry to leave the house. She didn't need much coaxing.

As she walked across the grass she felt something on her back. It was probably a bug. She twitched her shoulders but the feeling persisted. When they reached the trees in Dan's front yard Melinda turned around to check her shoulder. The attic window caught her eye. She gasped. There was a woman at the window looking down at her and the look on her face was as anguished as the soldier's.

Melinda made a strangled noise and pointed upward. Dan heard her and looked first at the window, then back at Melinda. "What? What's the matter?"

"There at the window." Kevin followed her pointing finger. Both boys stared back at Melinda.

"Don't you see her?" Melinda asked. Her voice felt funny, as though she had swallowed glue.

"What? What do you see?"

"A woman." But as Melinda spoke the clouds shifted and the figure was gone. "It was the figure of a woman and she had that same look that the soldier had."

"I didn't see anything," Kevin said.

"It was the ghost," Melinda said with certainty. "The woman at the window."

"Ghosts don't appear in the daytime," Kevin said. "Everybody knows that."

"I've read about ghosts that appear at different times during the day," Melinda told him. "I know it was a ghost."

"It could have been the light," Dan said.

"It wasn't. I saw her face. She's connected to our soldier. I'm sure of it. We have to go back and look." Melinda said these words but she didn't want to go back. She would rather do almost anything than go back. But she knew she had to. The woman's face had had a sense of urgency about it. Time seemed to matter to these ghosts. Reluctantly, Melinda turned around.

And just as she stepped up on the front porch, a car drove up. Dan's grandfather got out.

13

Melinda didn't stop to think. She leaped off the porch and ran until she reached the woods. She hid behind a thick oak and watched through the leaves of a holly bush. If Roy Sasser had noticed her flight, he gave no sign as he got out of the small gray car and slammed the door hard. He was wearing gray trousers and a tweed jacket with a blue shirt but no tie. His white beard was as pointed as it had been before. His heavy black eyebrows jutted down over his eyes.

"I thought you were going to be gone all day," Dan said.

"John's plane was delayed and he had to be rerouted through Baltimore," Mr. Sasser said.

He flicked a brief look at the boys from under those eyebrows. His glance lingered a moment on Kevin who stood like a post behind a rocking chair. Melinda thought Mr. Sasser was going to speak but he only shook his head slightly and went into the house.

Melinda wondered what he'd been about to say. He didn't look evil or scary, just mildly curious. Then she remembered what she'd seen on the stairs. He'd looked murderous then.

The boys stood on the porch. Were they waiting for her? Melinda wasn't going near that house. Not with that terrible man there. She waited behind the tree. Finally Kevin came looking for her.

"He didn't kill us," he said.

"Yet," Melinda said. Kevin hadn't seen how Roy Sasser had looked on the stairs.

"Dan's expecting us to come back."

Melinda looked at Dan still waiting on the porch. He had forgiven her once. She couldn't let him down again. She couldn't let the ghost down. Why had Roy Sasser terrorized her on the stairs? If he was antisocial, why had he gone to meet a friend at the airport? How did he even have a friend? Maybe he was only antisocial to kids.

She didn't know what to think about the man on the stairs. He had looked exactly like Dan's grandfather. But Dan said he wasn't home. Neither Dan nor Kevin had seen him in the attic. He'd appeared instantly after they went up so he couldn't have been hiding. He would have had to be waiting at the top of the stairs to come down in time to confront her, and the boys had sworn nobody was up there.

She felt sick. Her knees weren't noodle knees now, they were jelly knees. How could she go back in with him there? She watched Dan. He seemed to be looking straight at her through the thick leaves. She remembered the anguished faces of the ghosts. They were close to solving the mystery of their ghosts. She was sure of it. They couldn't stop now.

Melinda swallowed. This was the hardest thing she had ever had to do. "We have to go back," she said in a faint voice.

Kevin looked at her. "Come on."

Dan smiled at Melinda when they reached the porch. "I'm glad you came back," he said. "I told you Roy was OK. He's just a little gruff sometimes."

He was more than gruff. But this wasn't the time to argue. "I think we are running out of time," she said. "I think something is happening in their time. I could feel it when I saw the ghost in your window. Just stay close to me."

Dan led the way. Melinda heard the sound of water running in the kitchen as they went up the stairs. They were safe from Roy Sasser for now.

The attic rooms had grown hotter while they were outside. The boys attacked boxes that had been pushed back under the eaves. Melinda kept expecting Mr. Sasser to pop up from a box or from behind an old chair, although she knew it was silly. She must have imagined the man on the stairs. But she kept glancing over her shoulder until she heard the back door slam and the tractor start up out near the barn. She followed the sound as it moved away from the house and out into the orchards. Melinda walked over to the window. She pulled up a nearby chair. It was a wooden kitchen chair that had once been blue then painted white. Chips and dents showed the blue underneath. It seemed sturdy so she sat in it and stared at the room. In the afternoon light she could see that the walls had been papered a long time ago. The paper was yellowed with age but she could make out faded pink rosebuds and ribbons. A bed had been shoved under the sloping eaves, then piled with boxes. Someone had lived in the room at some time. You didn't put fancy paper on walls if an attic was only used for storage. Melinda wondered if the woman in the window had lived here.

"Was it you?" she whispered to the unknown woman. "Was this your room? Were you watching for the soldier to come back after the battle?"

There was no answer. Melinda heard only the scuffling, thumping, scraping noises the boys made as they moved and shoved and pawed through boxes and piles of old things. There were too many boxes, too many places where a tiny clue could be hidden forever and not enough time. They could organize the attic and go through it a section at a time, item by item. They could probably finish it by the end of the summer.

But that would be too late.

Where did those words come from? What put them in her head. Why did she feel a sense of urgency, that time was running out?

Melinda tried to imagine someone living in this attic room. What had it been like? Did she read up here at night while she waited for her soldier? Or whoever she waited for? There would have been a candlestand by the bed. Melinda shoved some boxes over but there was only a trunk against the wall next to the bed.

Sometimes when she read at night, Melinda often slid her book under the bed when she was too sleepy to read anymore. It was there waiting for her the next night when she went to bed. She got down on her knees and looked under the bed. She found a dog collar, a woman's black buttoned shoe, a riding crop, and a thriving colony of dust bunnies that made her sneeze three times. She used the riding crop to pull other things from under the bed. A book and a sewing kit in a frayed basket, more books. Melinda opened the basket eagerly, certain that this was where the clue lay. A woman of the Civil War period would have had a sewing kit. That would be the logical place for her to hide a clue. The stuffed satin lining had split with age into threads, the stuffing yellowed and matted. Inside she found a tarnished silver thimble and some bits of ribbon. No letters, no maps, no clues.

Disappointed, Melinda looked at the first book, *What Miss Mary Fancied*. She thumbed the thick pages. "Miss Mary loved her dear little teacloth. Aunt Fanny had embroidered it with dear little daisies and dear little pansies looking like dear little faces. . . ." *Eeuw*. How could anybody read such stuff? She checked the publication date. 1894. Too late. Melinda looked at the next one. More of the same. All of the books were awful and all had been published after the Civil War. She tossed the last one aside without even opening it. *Lady Castlemere's Fan*. What a silly title. Who wants to read about a fan?

Well, so much for her brainstorm. Melinda got up, ready to admit defeat.

No.

It wasn't a voice exactly, not even a whisper or a sound. It was more like the memory of a whisper. Melinda turned back. The window seat was empty.

"What is it? Did I miss something?"

She waited for a sign. The attic was silent except for the boys in the next room.

Melinda sighed and started over. She went through the sewing basket and all of the books, in case somebody had stuck something that held a clue between the pages. When she got to the last book she checked the front—1860, published in London. The book could have been here when their ghost was alive. Melinda felt a thrill. She held the book up to see if anything would fall out. Nothing. But in the front she found a bookplate printed in Latin that she couldn't read and the name Amanda Holroyd written in fancy script. And near the back somebody had written in the same small faded brown script in the margins and on the end pages.

"Dan! Kevin! I've found something. Come listen to this."

Melinda felt her fingertips tingle as she held the pages to the light and began to read. The script was tiny and crowded as though the writer knew there might not be enough room for all the words.

July 21, 1861

I write in the back of a book I know Father would not deign to touch as he deems Poetry, Essays, and Sermons the only fit matter for elevation of the mind. But Cora Lee gave this book to me on my last visit to her and he would not dare to speak against a Lee. My secrets will be safe with Lady Castlemere. I must open my Heart if only to book pages. This day has been the worst of my life and my Heart will burst if I do not unburden it somehow. The guns boomed their death knells throughout the long hot afternoon. When they stopped the air was as still as death. Birds had long ceased their song and left for safer climes. Mossy begged me to come to the cellar but I stayed by the attic window. The battle sounded as close as the Union camp on the other side of Holroyd Hill but it was in truth far away and there was no danger from its guns. I watched the smoke as it rose above the treetops in the distance and I thought about Daniel in That Hell and prayed that he would be Safe to come back to me.

July 22, 1861

I watched from the window all night. Mossy tried to get me to bed. I consented to remove my stays but would not leave the window. Sleep overcame my watch but dreams of the Battle wakened me. Daniel did not come. Father returned in the morning filled with joy for the Great Southern Victory. I should be glad but I am not. My Heart aches for Daniel. Father made us kneel and Pray for the Southern boys. I was able to do this but when he inveighed against the Yankee Devils, I merely moved my lips and let no sound escape. I cannot Pray for ill to befall my Daniel.

July 23, 1861

Father's jubilance is a Dagger in my Heart. The North is quaking with Terror. Washington lies in a helpless panic awaiting the Southern Invasion.

July 31, 1861

I slipped away to the Union camp while Father was in Broadfalls seeking news. All was in disarray. The officer I spoke with had no knowledge of Daniel. I fear the worst.

August 7, 1861

I cannot bear the waiting, the Unknown. If Daniel were not wounded nor a Prisoner, I know that he would Endeavor to send me word. The Confederates did not attack Washington. Father is livid. Mossy and I have stayed out of his Way all day but had to listen to him for an hour at Evening Prayers. I fear we would be at Prayer yet but I was overcome with faintness due to the Extreme Heat. I Pray for the relief of rain.

October 1, 1861

I can no longer hide my Condition. Father has locked me in this attic room. He says my Shame must be hidden from the World. He refuses to believe in my marriage to Daniel by the Chaplain. He went to the Union camp but the Chaplain was killed in the Battle and there is no word of Daniel. He does not know that I Willingly stay here by this window where I can see the road my Daniel will walk up when he returns to me. I can be happy no other place. Mossy brings me trays but I can hardly partake of enough nourishment so heavy is my Heart.

Christmas Day, 1861

I Pray for Daniel. Father allowed me to come downstairs for the Day spent mostly in Prayer. I went only because of the Babe. It was warm by the fire downstairs. I was allowed one cup of hot punch. Would that Daniel has as much Wherever he may be.

January 1, 1862

A new Year. I Pray that it will bring Daniel to me. I was ill all Day.

March 7, 1862

Mossy says that the Babe will come by Nightfall. I Pray so. I cannot go on."

"Wow," Kevin said.

Melinda stared at the fading script. She felt strangely connected to the writer. She touched the words with her fingers. She could almost feel the pen scratching them in secret so long ago.

"Is that all?" Dan asked.

Melinda flipped through the pages and nodded. "I think the baby was already coming when she wrote that. The writing on the March 7 entry is uneven."

"So what happened after that?" Dan asked.

"I think she died," Melinda said.

"You don't know that," Kevin said.

"A lot of women died in childbirth in those days," Dan said.

"I think she died without ever knowing what happened to her Daniel. That's why she is still watching from this window." As she said those words, Melinda became sure. She waited for Kevin to argue with her but he didn't.

"We need to find out who these people were," he said.

"The soldier's name was Daniel," Melinda said. She looked at Dan.

Kevin looked at him, too. And then without any basis in facts, he said, "I think they must have been Dan's ancestors."

"The initials on the pocket watch were DC," Melinda said.

Dan had a funny look on his face. Melinda thought he might faint this time. Instead he said, "This is really spooky, guys."

"Yeah, we know," Kevin said.

"No, I mean really really spooky. My initials are DC."

"But that's only because your mother married a man named Czernikow," Melinda said.

"I know. But why did they name me Daniel?"

"What's your father's name?" Kevin asked.

"Robert Augustus."

"Maybe it's a family name," Melinda suggested. "You could call your mother up at the library and ask her."

"She went to a meeting in Richmond."

Melinda swallowed. "You could ask your grandfather."

"He doesn't like to talk about family things."

Melinda wouldn't want to ask Roy about something he didn't want to talk about either. But he was Dan's grandfather. "It's important," she said.

They waited in the kitchen while Dan went to find Roy Sasser. The clock ticked steadily just as it or one like it had ticked that July day in 1861. She looked at the pottery animals on the mantel, the candlesticks and lanterns. The house didn't seem like the sort of house where such a mean man lived. It seemed very pleasant. But it had been the home of Amanda's father, too.

Kevin was standing by the fireplace. After a few minutes he said, "Look at this."

"What?"

He was staring intently at the mantel. Melinda looked over his shoulder at the lanterns on the mantle. Two were glass hurricane lanterns. But behind them stood a smaller one made of tin.

"Are you thinking what I'm thinking?" he asked.

"It looks like the one the soldier carries," Melinda said.

"Yeah, it does. But it's a common type. There were probably millions just like it. Now if you took prints and found the ghost's fingerprints on it . . ."

Melinda poked him in the ribs. "Don't be silly. But it could be the same lantern. One of the people who lived here could have found it and brought it here." Her voice trailed off. "The murderer could have brought it here."

14

Dan's face was pale and serious when he returned from talking to his grandfather.

"What did he say?" Kevin asked.

Dan didn't answer but went straight through to the hall. Melinda and Kevin followed, mystified. Dan opened the glass door of the middle bookcase and took out a big heavy book with a dark red, embossed leather cover.

"He said to look in here," Dan said as he heaved the book onto the table by the front door. "It's the family *Bible*. He said all the family is recorded in it."

The pages were thick. They crackled as Dan turned them. In the back of the *Bible* pages were marked Births, Deaths, and Marriages in fancy script. Dan ran his finger down the names. "It's here," he said. He pointed to a name under Births. "Daniel Holroyd born March 7, 1862."

Melinda stared at the name. It was real, all of it, the ghost, the words in margins of *Lady Castlemere's Fan*, the face in the window. She felt thrilled and shocked at the same time. It was wonderful and exciting to find out the truth but it was also scary.

"Amanda wrote that Mossy said the baby would be born on March 7 so that must be the one," Kevin said. "So he was your ancestor."

Melinda scanned the page but the script was hard to read in the shaded light of the hall. "What about his mother?" she asked. "What happened to Amanda?"

Dan turned the page. "Amanda Holroyd died March 9, 1862," Dan read. "She fits, too."

"She lived long enough to name him for his father," Melinda said.

"But she didn't convince her father that they were married," Kevin pointed out. "She's not listed under marriages."

"That's so sad." Tears came into Melinda's eyes. She brushed them away. It had happened so long ago. And yet she felt involved with their story, as if they were people that she knew. "She never found out what happened to her husband. He never knew that he had a son and his son didn't even have his name."

"No, they gave him his mother's surname," Dan said.

"Holroyd. You mean this hill and everything was named for your ancestors?" Kevin asked.

Dan nodded.

"But your grandfather's name is Sasser, not Holroyd. Roy Sasser."

"No, it's Holroyd Sasser. He was always called Roy. See, it's in here, too. The family has lived here since before the Civil War. Roy says there's a small old family graveyard at the end of the last orchard."

"A graveyard!" Melinda and Kevin spoke together.

"It didn't show up on the map at the library," Kevin added.

"The map ends in the middle of the orchards," Dan said.

"Why didn't you tell us?" Kevin demanded.

"I've never seen it. I didn't even know it was there." Dan put the *Bible* back on the shelf and closed the glass door. "Roy just told me. Anyway the ghost isn't going there."

"Let's go find it," Kevin said already halfway to the front door.

Melinda followed him out on the porch but hung back as Kevin jumped the steps.

"Come on," Dan prodded her.

"Your grandfather told us to stay away from his orchards."

"It's OK if you're with me. It's probably OK if you're not with me now that he knows about you."

Melinda wasn't as sure about that as Dan seemed to be. Dan hadn't been on the stairs that day. Roy Sasser seemed to have two different personalities. She didn't think she could stand another confrontation with him. He would surely make Dan stay away from her and Kevin.

....

THE graveyard was small and grown over with vines and weeds. It was easy to see why Dan had never noticed it. Three tumbled stone walls surrounded three graves. The fourth wall was part of the long wall at the end of the orchard. The graves were marked with old gravestones that leaned in different directions. They were splotched with moss and lichen and the carving on them had almost weathered away. Melinda knelt and pulled the wild roses, blackberry vines, and Virginia creeper away. She traced the name of Amanda Holroyd on the smallest one.

The other two stones were those of Amanda's parents Quentin Holroyd and Martha Hunter Holroyd.

"Now we know who haunts your house," Melinda said. She sat down on the orchard wall beside Dan. "And we know why."

"Not exactly," Kevin corrected her. "We know that Amanda was waiting for her husband to return from the Battle of Manassas. And we know that he was on his way to her. But we still don't know why he didn't get there."

"Maybe it doesn't matter why he didn't get there. Maybe this is where he's trying to go every night. Maybe if we bury his bones here in her grave, their ghosts will be together for the rest of eternity and he can stop walking," Melinda said. "And she can stop watching from the window."

"You mean just get a shovel and dig a hole in Amanda's grave and put the bones in?" Dan asked.

"Yeah. And we should do it right at midnight," Kevin said with a ghoulish grin, "just at the time that Daniel's ghost disappears."

"I didn't mean that," Melinda began.

"But it might be the only way it will work," Dan said slowly.

"What do you mean?" Kevin asked.

"Do you remember the date of the first entry in the book?"

"Sometime in July," Kevin said.

"July 21. And the date today is?"

Melinda's stomach felt like it was going down in a fast elevator to her ankles.

Kevin checked his digital watch. "Today is July 21."

Nobody spoke. Kevin leaned against the wall. He picked a ripe blackberry, popped it into his mouth, noticed where it was growing, and spat it out. Dan stared off through the orchard.

Melinda bit her lip. "This is the reason the ghosts seemed so desperate. Time is running out on them," she said.

"Right. If we don't get them together tonight, it might be their last chance," Dan said turning back to them.

"You don't know that," Kevin objected. "There aren't any rules about that stuff."

"There could be and we just don't know them," Dan said.

Kevin gave in. "OK. I vote that we bury them this afternoon in nice friendly broad daylight," he said.

"You're just scared to do it at night," Melinda said.

"I don't see why it has to be at night, that's all."

"Do we all agree that Daniel's and Amanda's ghosts are the ones we've been seeing?" Melinda asked.

"We agree about Daniel," Kevin said.

"You're the only one who has seen Amanda," Dan reminded her. "You and possibly Great-aunt Hannah."

"OK. We've solved the mystery of who they are and why their ghosts are walking. I think we have to finish this ourselves and bury Daniel's bones tonight," Melinda said.

"Let's vote on it," Kevin said, jumping up. "All those in favor of this afternoon raise your hands." He raised his right hand.

Melinda and Dan looked at him.

"OK, OK." He slumped back against the wall. "Midnight it is. I don't see why, but I'll do it. But maybe we should tell our parents."

"No." Melinda and Dan spoke together.

"They might not understand," Dan said.

"They might try to stop us or insist that we call the police or something and then it would be too late," Melinda said. "That's what you were hoping, wasn't it?"

"No, no. I want to do what's best for our ghosts," Kevin

said. "But it is probably illegal not to report human bones to the police."

"Probably. But who would believe our story?" Melinda said. She put her hands flat on the wall. The stones felt warm against her palms. No cold here. They were safe.

"Nobody. They would think we were bananas," Dan said.

"Maybe we are," Kevin said.

15

Do you think they're going to watch TV all night?" Melinda asked Kevin. They were in his room waiting for Mom and Phil to turn off the TV and go to sleep.

"No, not all night. They're probably watching an old movie." Kevin checked his watch. "It's almost 11:30. We can't wait any longer. Let's go, but be quiet." He slid off the edge of his bed and went to the door.

Melinda closed her comic book. *Ghost Mountain*. It wasn't half as interesting as the real thing. "What if they check on us?"

"They won't if your light is off. Did you put a dummy in your bed like I told you?"

"Yes, but I don't think it will fool Mom." She'd used Gwendolyn for the hair. It was neat and stiff, unlike Melinda's floppy hair and not even the right color but it was the best she could do. They hadn't taken this much care the other times they'd slipped out at night. But Mom and Phil had already gone to bed then and were unlikely to check. If Mom opened Melinda's door for some reason and saw her asleep, she would tiptoe back to her room without turning on the light.

They were taking more care this time because they were going to a graveyard to bury someone, someone that Melinda felt was almost a friend or family member. It wasn't something you just ran out and did, like following a ghost. This was serious.

"Where's Raj?"

"He's in my room, sleeping." Raj hadn't been happy to be left behind. "I still think we should take him."

"No." Kevin shook his head. "If they do check and he's gone, they'll know you've gone somewhere and they'll probably call the police."

It was true. Raj had slept with her since he was a puppy. He thought it was his job to protect Melinda. She wished he were going with them again to protect her tonight. She missed his warm furry presence, the wet slurps of his big tongue.

"Let's go." Kevin eased his door open.

The hall was quiet. Melinda could hear muffled TV sounds behind Mom and Phil's door. She crept down the stairs after Kevin and grabbed him in the kitchen.

"Did you get the box out of the garage?"

"No. I never had a chance. Phil was in there looking for a screwdriver when I went to do it. I was afraid he was going to open the box but he found the screwdriver before he got to that shelf. We'll have to get it now."

"Well, go on then," Melinda said.

"You go."

"No, you."

"Come on, we'll both go."

Melinda held the flashlight while Kevin took the box off the shelf. The garage seemed different in the dark, scarier and the things in it took on a sinister look—the hulking station wagon with its teethlike grille, bared in a steely grimace; the garden tools hanging on their hooks like weapons on the walls; the coil of bicycle chain on the floor, ready to strike.

"Bring the shovel," Kevin said holding the box of bones out in front of him. Melinda stifled a giggle. "The bones won't bite you."

"Here, you carry them."

For answer Melinda eased the shovel off its hook. They slipped out of the garage and headed down the old road.

The night was dark and loud with the sounds of crickets and frogs. Clouds hung over the moon. The leaves seemed to suck up what light there was. Melinda used the flashlight and told herself it was the same road they had walked over before many times, there was nothing to be afraid of, stop imagining things, don't think about ghosts, just remember Daniel and Amanda and their sad doomed romance.

They rounded the curve where they had found the bones and saw a light just as something hooted nearby. Melinda jumped.

The light was Dan. "It was only an owl," he said flashing his light over the woods.

The trees seemed to hover over them as if ready to grab them. Why was this night so different from the other nights when they had waited for the ghost? Melinda wished again she had brought Raj. She felt uneasy, as if something could go wrong. But she was sure burying the bones in the graveyard would reunite Daniel and Amanda. It was the sort of ghost behavior she had read about. And they had to do it tonight, the anniversary of the Battle of Manassas. Melinda tried to reason away her misgivings but they just wouldn't go away.

Dan put his flashlight in his back pocket. He took the shovel from her and held her hand so that Kevin couldn't see and tease them. She smiled through the dark and he squeezed her hand. Maybe it would be all right. Maybe all three of them together could do it. Melinda thought Kevin looked like he would like to hold their hands, too. But his arms were around the box of bones.

They waited on the old road for Daniel's ghost to walk down it just as he had nearly a hundred and fifty years before on July 21, making his painful way back to Amanda after the terror of the battle and the pain of his wound. Melinda didn't think she could bear to look at his sad face one more time. She concentrated on what they expected to accomplish tonight. If all went as they had planned, she would never see him again. Daniel's ghost would be reunited with Amanda. And maybe this time she would see the anguish erased from his face and a look of peace on it.

"What time is it?" she asked Kevin.

He put the box down on the road and illuminated the digits on his watch. "11:45. He should be here any minute now."

But they had to wait for Daniel's ghost to shuffle through the house and along the road. He reached them just before midnight. They could see the light from his lantern moving slowly along the road. Melinda felt herself tremble with excitement. She squeezed Dan's hand. Kevin picked up the box.

"OK, let's go to the graveyard."

"Will he follow us?" Melinda asked. She didn't want to make any mistakes. Their plan had to work.

"I don't know. There aren't any rules, remember. We'll just have to try it," Kevin said.

"I think we ought to wait," she said.

Dan let Melinda's hand go as he went ahead to light the way to the graveyard. Kevin followed, then Melinda. They passed the track to Dan's house and the orchard where Melinda and Kevin had met his grandfather. The stones of the wall were a dull silvery gray in the meager light from the veiled moon. Dan ran his flashlight across them, over the headstones, the briery graves.

Kevin put the box down. "Let's get this digging over with."

Melinda turned to look down the road. It was dark through the trees. She could see a light in her house but no lights in Dan's and no following light on the road. "He isn't coming," she whispered.

"We can't wait," Kevin said. "Give me the shovel."

"What if this doesn't work?" Melinda persisted. "Daniel's ghost should be here by now."

"We're giving it our best shot," Kevin said.

"If it doesn't work, there's nothing we can do about it," Dan said.

"We have to do something about it. It's not your house that a ghost walks through," Melinda reminded him.

"No, it's just my great-great-great-great-grandfather walking around the neighborhood and my great-great-great-great grandmother sitting in the attic window waiting for him."

"You're right. But I still think we should wait a little longer," Melinda said.

"What for?" Kevin put his foot on the shovel.

"I don't know," Melinda said miserably. How could she explain a feeling she couldn't even describe, like there was a precipice in the darkness that they were going to step over? The owl chose that moment to hoot again nearby. It was a lonely, mournful sound. All three jumped.

"That does it. I'm not waiting a minute longer." Kevin grabbed the shovel and stuck it into the briers on Amanda's grave. He scooped out a pile of dirt. "We're going to do this and get out of here."

Melinda kept watch by the road. The moon looked ghostly behind the thick clouds. The woods were dark, the only light came from Dan's flashlight. Behind she heard the shovel bite into the earth as Kevin dug deeper.

"How deep do you think it should be?" he asked.

"A foot or two," Dan said. "The point of burying was to keep wild animals from digging up the dead. I don't think the raccoons around here will bother with bones this old."

Melinda strained to see the bobbing light from Daniel's lantern but the road remained black and impenetrable as Kevin's digging took on a rhythm.

Then suddenly he stopped digging. Kevin made a strangled sound. Melinda turned back to tell him that the hole should be deep enough to get Daniel close to Amanda but the words caught in her throat as she saw what the boys were staring at in frozen horror.

As she watched, a terrible figure rose out of the grave of Quentin Holroyd, slowly, slowly, upward, upward until it loomed over them, a stark, black-clad figure of a man, its beard pointed and white, its bushy black eyebrows set in a ferocious scowl over the evilest black eyes Melinda had ever seen. It looked like Dan's grandfather, Roy Sasser, but it wore the clothes of Abraham Lincoln's time. The figure held a long gun. Light glinted on the barrel. It was pointed at them.

16

*T*ime seemed to stand still. Melinda couldn't move. Her feet had turned to stone. She tried to scream but her throat was paralyzed. She wanted to look away but her eyes were locked. And she was cold. The sinkhole cold was like desert heat compared to the cold surrounding them now. She felt embedded in a block of ice. Those eyes burned through the cold with the laser intensity of hate.

"Who—who is that?" Kevin's voice cracked. He seemed to be having trouble breathing.

The ghost didn't seem to hear Kevin's words. He stared at them, through them. Suddenly Melinda realized that he wasn't even looking at them. She found her voice.

"It's Quentin Holroyd. I don't think he can see us," she whispered. "He seems to be looking through us." Her voice sounded strange in her ears, as though she were wearing earmuffs. But at least her teeth weren't chattering. Much.

"Behind us. He's looking behind us," Dan said through clenched teeth. "There's something behind us."

Now Melinda could see the light. It wasn't from their flash-lights or the moon. Icy prickles ran down her spine. She felt like something was clawing the back of her neck. Something awful was about to happen. They had to move, to get away, to try to stop that horrible apparition.

"He's a ghost," Melinda said. "He can't shoot us."

"That's a possibility," Kevin agreed. "But I don't think we should take that chance."

"We can't stay here," Dan said. "Let's all move left at the same time on the count of three. One, two, three."

They dived into the darkness beside them. They clutched each other, dropping their flashlights. The gun didn't go off. When Melinda turned around it was still pointed where they had been standing. But now she could see what had been behind them. It was the ghost of Daniel. His lantern cast the only light in the blackness. It fell in long streaks across the bearded ghost's black coat and slashed across his terrible face, those dark hooded eyes, the eyes that had blazed at her with hate on the stairs to Dan's attic and she knew who he was. It hadn't been Roy Sasser that day at all. The man on the stairs was that awful ghost of Quentin Holroyd coming after her the way he must have all those years ago if Amanda went down-stairs without his permission.

Melinda was shaking now. Kevin clutched her arm on one side, Dan on the other. They shook together in a collective hug as the ghosts faced each other.

It seemed important to Melinda to speak. Her words came stumbling out. She thought they needed to be said to clarify what had happened all those years ago, to say them aloud in the presence of the two ghosts. "Daniel came b-back to Amanda after the b-battle," Melinda said. "It took him a long t-time because of his wounded leg. He came back but he met her father instead and now he's going to shoot Daniel."

"He's already done it," Dan said. He sounded calmer. "Maybe he's been doing it forever, every night."

"We have to stop him," Melinda said.

"We can't stop a ghost," Kevin said.

Melinda knew he was right. Neither of the ghosts had ever seemed to notice them. Except on the stairs. But even then Quentin Holroyd might have thought Melinda was Amanda. And that time Daniel had looked into her eyes—he could have thought she was Amanda, too. Both ghosts seemed to be stuck in the pattern of what had happened that night. That was why Daniel always stopped at the spot where he had been killed. But tonight he hadn't stopped. He was here at the graveyard. The bones must have brought him here. Just as they had brought his killer.

"Quentin Holroyd," she whispered.

Kevin kicked her. "Don't make him notice us," he said.

But as he spoke the ghost swung his head toward them.

"Oh, no," Kevin groaned.

Quentin Holroyd turned the gun at them. Melinda could see the black hole of the barrel. Inside that hole was death.

"He's going to shoot," Dan gasped.

"He can't do that," Kevin said, his voice going up and down. "Can he?"

Daniel's ghost moved, distracting Quentin Holroyd. He aimed the gun at Daniel again. There was resolution in his face, that terrible face of a man who thought he was judge of everyone. Quentin Holroyd's finger tightened on the trigger.

"He's going to shoot Daniel!" Melinda didn't know what would happen if Quentin Holroyd shot Daniel here instead of the place where the original murder took place but she thought it would somehow end Daniel's chances for eternal peace. They couldn't stop Quentin Holroyd. There was only one hope.

"Amanda! Amanda!" she screamed.

A mist floated upward out of the hole Kevin had dug. The mist swirled into the shape of a woman wearing a long full-skirted dress. She looked at Daniel and they moved to each other as though they hadn't been parted for over a hundred years. The pain lifted from the soldier's face, his brow smoothed, his eyes cleared, then reflected happiness. He reached for her and then as they embraced, their shapes slowly began to dissolve over Amanda's grave.

Quentin Holroyd's face contorted with rage. His mouth twisted into a horrible snarl, his eyes bulged. He began to turn from the dissolving mist that had been Daniel and Amanda.

"Let's get out of here!" Kevin yelled.

They ran holding hands, forgetting the flashlights, forgetting the shovel, forgetting the box of bones, leaving Quentin Holroyd alone in his murderous fury. Melinda only wanted to get back to the safety of her house where there were lights and the noise of the TV and Raj's familiar furry warmth.

Dan came with them. "I don't want to go home in the dark tonight," he said.

"You can spend the night with us but won't your mom be mad if she finds out?" Kevin asked when they reached the back deck.

"She's still in Richmond and Roy won't notice." Melinda didn't blame him for not wanting to go to that house tonight. What if Quentin appeared on the stairs or in his room? She shuddered and pushed the image of the horrible ghost away.

They fortified themselves with a box of chocolate chip

cookies and a quart of milk as they went through the kitchen. Melinda got glasses and they went up to Kevin's room.

The light was off in Mom's room and she could hear Phil snoring faintly. It was a comforting sound. She opened her door and called Raj to come in with them. They sat on the floor and she hugged Raj before giving him his cookie.

Melinda waited for the boys to mention the ghost. Kevin flipped through the channels on his TV and found an old movie with Nelson Eddy and Jeanette MacDonald. Nobody spoke. The room was filled with the sounds of munching cookies and the movie. Nelson Eddy and his band of men sang, "Stout-hearted Men" and Melinda felt safe.

By the time the movie ended and Jeanette and Nelson were together singing forever, she was sleepy and ready to tumble into her bed. But something was in it, something with horrible frozen-faced staring eyes. She jerked back the covers.

It was only Gwendolyn. She had forgotten putting the doll in her bed. She called Raj who didn't need to be asked twice to jump up and snuggle with her. She left the light on beside her bed and stared at the circle it made on her ceiling stirred by the paddles of the overhead fan into flickering shadow patterns. She did not want to remember how the ghost of Quentin Holroyd had looked as Daniel and Amanda disappeared together.

There was something else she didn't want to remember. Melinda pushed all thought of the night away and concentrated on Raj. She blinked her eyes once and then it was morning, a fresh breeze blowing her curtains around in a slow dance. She could hear birds twittering. The sun washed away the ghosts of the night before. But Melinda knew she would never forget any of it.

....

"WE have to go back and finish what we started," she announced when Kevin and Dan wandered out on the deck laden with bowls of cereal and tall glasses of orange juice.

"Do we have to?" Kevin crunched his cereal.

"Yeah, and we better do it before Roy discovers that box of bones," Dan said.

"I forgot about that," Kevin said. "Those bones are in a box with our address on it. If someone finds them and calls the police, we could have a hard time explaining it all."

"They'd never believe us," Dan said.

"Come on then," Melinda said. She jumped up and rinsed her cereal bowl and put it in the dishwasher. Raj leaped up, his eyes pleading. "OK, boy. Come on."

Dan's flashlight was still sending its beam invisibly into the sunlight but Melinda's had burned out. The only remains of the frightening visitation were the shovel and the half-dug hole. Dan picked up the shovel and thrust it into the hole.

"You would think that the ground would be marked somehow where the ghosts were," Melinda said. "Scorchmarks or a silvery X or something. Especially where . . ." Her voice trailed off. She didn't want to mention Quentin Holroyd's name, not even in the safety of the sunlit daytime.

But the leaves of the wild climbing roses and blackberries and creepers were unmarked. They weren't even mashed down, except where Melinda and the boys had pushed them aside out of their way. "Did we really see that last night?" she wondered aloud.

"I know what I saw," Kevin said. "Quentin Holroyd was about to shoot Daniel but Amanda appeared when you yelled her name and they disappeared together."

"That was who I saw on the stairs," Melinda said. "It wasn't Roy that day. It was," she dropped her voice, "Quentin Holroyd. Roy looks like him."

"No wonder you were scared," Dan said.

"I wouldn't have gone up those stairs again if I'd seen *that*," Kevin said.

"I wonder what happened to him," Melinda said.

There was a sudden hush. Dan stopped digging. Raj got to his feet. Melinda stared at her dog. His hackles stood up in a sharp line along the ridge of his back.

"I think this hole is deep enough," Dan said. "Get the box."

Melinda rubbed her arms. The sun was still bright but the cold seemed to be seeping upward from Quentin's grave. She stamped her feet.

Kevin stooped to pick up the box of bones and stayed there as if the box were too heavy to lift. His blue eyes were wide with shock. Melinda followed their gaze. The cold swirled around them.

Quentin rose from the mist on his grave and stood over Kevin pointing the gun at his heart, the evil angry eyes fastened on Kevin's face. He was looking at Kevin. He could see Kevin. He was going to shoot her brother. Or worse. The ghost advanced on Kevin.

Melinda didn't think she could move. The numbing cold had taken charge of her. Her throat was closing. She turned to run before it was too late.

This is what he wants. The voice seemed to hang in the mist, a whisper, a thought, a hint. Melinda didn't know where the words had come from.

She stopped in midrun. No. She wouldn't run this time. She faced the ghost of Quentin Holroyd.

"No," she screamed aloud. "You get away from my brother." With great effort she snatched up the box of bones and dumped them into the hole. "Sorry, Daniel," she whispered.

Quentin Holroyd's eyes blazed with rage. He opened his hideous mouth. Melinda tried to back away.

"No," she screamed again. "Nononononooooo." Her voice turned into an animal sound. "Get away, you monster!" She leaped at the ghost of Quentin Holroyd, swinging her clenched fists.

Quentin Holroyd aimed the gun at her. Kevin scrambled to his feet and stood beside her. Dan threw the shovelful of dirt. The clods fell through Quentin Holroyd who laughed evilly and advanced on the three.

17

Raj!" Melinda shouted.

Raj bared his fangs. A growl rumbled in his throat. It sounded like thunder. Dan brought the shovel down. It sliced through the ghostly gun. At the same time Raj sprang for Quentin Holroyd's throat. The ghost opened his mouth again to make a horrible sound. His eyes seemed to bore into Melinda's. Raj passed through him. The ghost fell back, his mouth open in rage. His eyes left Melinda and seemed to focus on something behind her. Melinda turned around and saw Daniel and Amanda, their fingers pointed at Quentin Holroyd, their faces stern and unyielding. Whatever power Quentin Holroyd had had in life and as a ghost over Daniel and Amanda was not strong enough to withstand them together. The gun left its target as the particles that were Quentin Holroyd's ghost dissipated over his grave. In seconds he was gone.

Immediately the cold went away. As Melinda, Kevin, and Dan watched, the heavy opaque mist broke into icy particles and then faded. Amanda and Daniel were still there. Amanda's eyes looked into Melinda's. Understanding seemed to flow between them. Melinda was sure Amanda smiled at her, a small Mona Lisa smile and Melinda knew it had been her voice whispering to Melinda through time just as she had beckoned to Melinda from the attic window. And then they were gone, quickly dissolving in a soft shimmer of particles that caught the sunlight with a flash of rainbow color. For a moment, Melinda wondered if she had imagined it all. She looked at Dan and Kevin and knew that she hadn't.

"They came back to save us," she said softly. "They came back one more time. It must have taken a lot of power to do that." Her ghost book said that appearing required a lot of energy for ghosts. She had thought theirs was all used up the night before.

"Yeah. I guess it's over," Kevin said.

But it wasn't over. Melinda wondered if anything was ever over. Quentin Holroyd had killed his son-in-law and ruined Amanda's life. He had condemned Daniel Holroyd to a lifetime of bastardy, a shameful secret in the nineteenth century. Who knows how all that had affected his descendants. Maybe that was why Roy Sasser was almost a hermit, she thought. The family had kept to itself and passed that behavior down. Melinda was glad Dan and his mother weren't like that.

They finished burying the bones, and silently walked back to the house. Phil was working on his fish. The basement doors were open. Melinda could hear the ring of his chisel. Raj pranced onto the deck as they sprawled in the chairs. Melinda bent over to give him a hug. His fur was warm from the sun and smelled nice and doggyish. She looked up at her brother and Dan and wondered how to tell them what they had to do.

"Um, guys, there's one more thing we have to do. We have to find out Daniel's last name."

Maybe if Phil weren't her stepfather, she wouldn't have thought about it. But maybe she would. It seemed right. Like dotting *i*'s and crossing *t*'s and putting one's dishes in the dishwasher. A gravestone should have the proper names cut into it.

Kevin groaned.

Dan looked wary. "Do we have to?"

Melinda nodded emphatically. "Yes, we do. We have to make sure that these ghosts don't walk anymore. If we put their names on the grave, then it will be sort of official. I liked Daniel after I got to know him and I think I could have been friends with Amanda. But I don't ever want to see Quentin Holroyd again."

Nobody did. The next day they rode Metro to downtown Washington, got off at the Mall, and walked across it to the National Archives. The desk guard looked at them suspiciously when they asked which floor the Civil War records were on, but he looked at everybody that way. They signed in and took the slow old-fashioned elevator up.

"How do we know who we're looking for?" Kevin had argued against going.

"We know his name was Daniel and his last name began with a *c*. He was in the Union army. That should narrow our search," Melinda said.

"And he disappeared after the first Battle of Manassas," Dan added.

It took longer than they had expected. They had to go all the way through the *c* microfilm before they found a soldier missing after Manassas. But they found him.

"Daniel Curtis," Dan said, "Columbia County, New York, enlisted, age 20, Fifty-first Regiment, New York."

Melinda stared at the matter-of-fact listing. She had the same feeling she'd had looking at Dan's family *Bible*. It was all real. They hadn't imagined it, Daniel, Amanda, Quentin. The ghosts had been real people just like her and Kevin and Dan. They'd breathed and laughed and cried. They had combed their hair and washed their faces, run, played. They'd had sorrows. A lot of sorrows. But they'd had dreams, too, and happiness.

Kevin cut into her thoughts. "Now that that's solved let's go over to the Air and Space Museum across the Mall," he suggested.

Melinda was torn. She wanted to see the rocks at the Natural History Museum. "We can come back to the Mall," she said. "But I think we should go home and really finish this so that Quentin Holroyd won't show himself ever again."

"Let's vote," Kevin said. "All those in favor of staying at the museums, raise your hands." Kevin raised his hand.

Melinda and Dan looked at each other. "I think we should go back," Dan said.

"All right, all right. But I'm coming down here tomorrow," Kevin grumbled.

Melinda didn't think he really minded going home. The thought of seeing Quentin again was enough to spoil anybody's day at the museums. And there was one final thing they had to do to end Daniel Curtis's ordeal.

They were quiet on the Metro back to Broadfalls. No one spoke as they unchained their bikes at the station.

After Dan delivered his papers, Kevin borrowed a mallet, chisel, and goggles from Phil and they went back to the grave-yard. Melinda brought along a red marking pen.

She marked the leaning headstone and they took turns chiseling in the letters. The stone was worn and easily worked.

"Let's get it deep enough," Kevin said, "so that it won't wear off for at least a hundred years."

When they finished, Melinda traced the letters—"Daniel Curtis 1841–July 21, 1861 of the Fifty-first, New York, Amanda Holroyd Curtis, 1845–1862, wife of Daniel. There, that ought to take care of Quentin Holroyd."

"Yeah." Dan didn't look happy.

"What's the matter?" Melinda asked.

Dan picked up a pebble and threw it at Quentin Holroyd's gravestone. "It's awful to have a person like that for a great-great-great-great-great-grandfather," Dan said. "I mean he was a murderer. He killed my great-great-great-great-grandfather. And maybe caused his daughter's death."

"I guess he was," Melinda said. "But it was wartime. They were on different sides. He probably didn't think that way. He probably thought he was helping the Confederacy."

"Yeah, I guess so," Dan said.

"And Amanda might have died anyway. A lot of women did in those days," Melinda added.

"Maybe," Dan said.

"Besides, nobody is responsible for his ancestors," Kevin pointed out.

"No," Melinda agreed, thinking of Roy Sasser. His life had been affected by what had happened in 1861, things that weren't his fault either.

On the way back to the house they detoured by the sinkhole. Melinda wanted to see if the feeling of cold was still there. They stood around the depression amidst the excavated rocks. Melinda listened for the strange silence that came with the cold. Birds chirped in a nearby tree. The cicadas were louder than ever. Melinda thought she heard a frog somewhere. The sun's rays fell in uninterrupted warmth around them. Melinda smiled. She felt safe and at peace, the way she hoped Daniel and Amanda felt. The haunting of Holroyd Hill was over. Quentin Holroyd wasn't coming back here. He had no reason to now. Daniel Curtis would never walk through their house again so Quentin Holroyd couldn't shoot him. Amanda wouldn't haunt the attic now so Quentin couldn't keep her penned up there. He had no agenda, as Kevin would say.

When they reached the house, Kevin went to the garage to put the box that had held the bones out by the curb for the trashmen to pick up the next day. He said he didn't want to keep a box around that had had a person's bones in it, even if the person had been a good ghost. Dan was keeping the bag with the personal things, the watch, buttons, buckle. Melinda and Dan went on to the back deck. She thought she was going to like living on Holroyd Hill.

A basket of rose and green pears sat on the edge of the deck, a note tucked into the middle. It was addressed in a large black determined scrawl to Ms. Melinda Ryan.

"That's Roy's handwriting," Dan said as Melinda plucked it out of the shiny pears.

Melinda felt her nerves jump. She opened the note. "Nobody answered at the front so I brought the basket to the back. These are my earliest sweet pears. I developed the trees myself. I call them Holroyds. I hope they may win you over to un-tropical fruit. Next we'll try apples." The note was signed Roy Sasser.

"Why would my grandfather want to win you over to un-tropical fruit? What does that mean anyway?"

"Oh, um, I told him once that I didn't like apples and pears.

It was that first day when we met him in the orchard," Melinda said explaining only halfway.

"Yeah, but untropical fruit?"

"I told him I only eat tropical fruit."

"Oh. Well. I guess it's his way of apologizing for yelling at you that day."

Melinda bit into a pear. It was deliciously sweet. "I've never had one ripe off a tree before. I think I like pears," she said, chewing. "I'll write him a note."

"You could come over and tell him yourself," Dan said. "He won't bite. He's really a nice grandfather. He always has time for me when I ask him something. He takes me fishing and he's teaching me about growing things."

Melinda laughed. "My mom always makes me write thank-you notes."

They sat on the edge of the deck. Melinda offered Dan a pear.

"No, thanks. I get plenty of those at home." He grinned. "We have everything you can think of made with apples and pears—cakes, muffins, stews, pies, jam, chutney, butter, baked, boiled, even fried."

Melinda tried to imagine fried pears.

Dan picked up a small rock by the steps and tossed it into the woods. "Want to go down to the stream and look for fossils?" he asked.

"That's only my favorite thing in the world to do," Melinda said, jumping off the edge of the deck.

"I thought it was discovering ghosts," Dan teased.

"I think I've discovered enough ghosts. For this year, anyway."

Raj's tail thumped the deck hopefully. "OK, come on, boy."

Raj leaped down and ran ahead, barking happily. "Let's go over to your house first," Melinda said. "I want to thank your grandfather in person."

Dan turned around to look at her. "Are you sure?"

"Of course, I'm sure." She tossed her hair back. She wasn't afraid of Roy Sasser now that he had written her such a nice note and given her the pears, now that she knew he was not the ogre that had menaced her on the stairs that day.

"OK," Dan said, grinning.

"But I'll still write him a note," she added.

They were halfway to the edge of the woods when Kevin came back from putting the box out by the street. "Hey, where are you going?"

Melinda told him.

"Can I come?" Kevin asked.

Melinda looked at Dan. He shrugged.

"Sure," she said. Then added under her breath, "This time."

Curtis Farm Road
East Chatham, NY 12060

August, 19-

Dear Dan, Melinda, and Kevin,

I was so pleased to receive your letter. How clever of you to call the library to find out if there were any Curtises still in the area. And what a story you had to tell!

I am the historian for the Curtis family. Daniel Curtis was my great-great-grandfather's brother. The family never knew what had happened to him in the war. We have never believed that he deserted but that he was killed somehow. How wonderful to find out the truth after almost a century and a half and that he left descendants. I am happy to welcome our new cousins to the family. I appreciate the pictures you sent and hope to make a trip South soon to visit the Manassas Battlefield and meet my new relatives and their friends.

I have completed the Civil War section of the Curtis family history and will send a copy to you as soon as it is printed.

Sincerely,

Maria Curtis Sherrill

Brenda Seabrooke began *The Haunting of Holroyd Hill* when she lived in a new house built over an old pre–Civil War road in Falls Church, Virginia. Her family heard strange, unexplained noises that sounded like footsteps moving through the house. She imagined that they were ghosts, and this is the story she wrote about them. Ms. Seabrooke is also the author of *The Bridges of Summer*, *Judy Scuppernong*, and other books for young readers. She lives in West Virginia.